FROM: _NustartFIB@go2outer.net_
SUBJECT: Upgrade

A message to our Earth Friends:

Sector Commander Miraz has retired. I am the new commander of Rigel Sector. In recognition of the good work being undertaken by Friends agents on Earth, your connection to the Outernet has been up-graded. You can find out more by logging on.

Here are your instructions:

1. Start reading this book. The first password is the name of Zodiac's ship.

2. Log on to the Outernet by typing _www.go2outer. net_ into your Internet browser, then enter this password to begin your adventure.

3. Enter your agent ID if you are already a Friend, or register as a new Friend with the FIB.

Remember to open all your o-mails and explore your FIB Files and Links — this is important.

Enjoy your new connection — let's hope it doesn't get taken over by the FOEs! Keep smart, keep safe.

Commander Nustart
Sector Commander, Rigel Sector
FIB (Friends Intelligence Bureau)

**Introducing something truly
out of this world . . .**

OUTERNET™

WWW.GO2OUTER.NET

the hunt

Steve Barlow and Steve Skidmore

AN
APPLE
PAPERBACK

SCHOLASTIC INC.
New York Toronto London Auckland Sydney
Mexico City New Delhi Hong Kong Buenos Aires

ISBN 0-439-43018-6

Published by Scholastic Inc., 557 Broadway, New York, NY 10012.
The Chicken House is published in the United States
in association with Scholastic Inc.

12 11 10 9 8 7 6 5 4 3 2 1   3 4 5 6 7 8/0

Printed in the U.S.A.   40
First Scholastic printing, May 2003

FIB ORIENTATION FILE:
FRIENDS INTELLIGENCE BUREAU

THIS IS A TOP-SECURITY-PROTECTED FILE FOR FRIENDS EYES ONLY. THIS INFORMATION MUST NOT BE COPIED, DUPLICATED, OR REVEALED TO ANY BEING NOT VERIFIED AS A FRIEND OF THE OUTERNET.

)(**Info Byte 1 — The Outernet:** The pan-galactic web of information. Created by The Weaver for the free exchange of information between all advanced beings in the Galaxy.

)(**Info Byte 2 — The Server:** Alien communication device and teleportation portal. The last such device in the hands of the Friends of the Outernet.

)(**Info Byte 3 — Friends:** Forces who are loyal to The Weaver in the struggle to free the Outernet from the clutches of The Tyrant.

)(**Info Byte 4 — FOEs:** The Forces of Evil, creatures loyal to The Tyrant, who seek to use the Outernet to control and oppress the people of the Galaxy.

- ℵ **Info Byte 5 — Bitz and Googie:** Shape-shifting aliens disguised as a dog and a cat, respectively. Bitz is a Friends agent (code-named Sirius) and ally of Janus. Googie (code-named Vega) was formerly a FOEs agent but claims now to be loyal to the Friends.

- ℵ **Info Byte 6 — Janus:** A Friends agent who, while trying to keep The Server away from the FOEs, disappeared into N-space.

- ℵ **Info Byte 7 — Jack Armstrong:** A fourteen-year-old human from England who became responsible for the fate of The Server when it was given to him as a birthday present. **Merle Stone** and **Lothar (Loaf) Gelt:** Jack's American friends from the nearby U.S. Air Force base who have been helping him keep The Server safe from the FOEs.

- ℵ **Info Byte 8 — Tracer:** The Tyrant's chief of surveillance, who tried to take The Server for his own purposes and is now on the run.

- ℵ **Info Byte 9 — Zodiac Hobo:** Space hippie and self-proclaimed desperado; gave Jack and friends a lift in his spaceship *Trigger*.

PROLOGUE

Secret Headquarters of The Tyrant, the Forbidden Sector

Bugs are among the most feared creatures in the Galaxy. Their muscle-bound, thick-skinned gray bodies and serious lack of social responsibility cause high levels of anxiety, stress, and agony wherever they appear.

Eyeball-popping razor-toothed ear-drillers from the planet Aaaaaargh! (with six *a*'s) are also high on the list of beings most likely to make a life-form's tentacles turn to jelly and antennae tie themselves in knots, along with an embarrassing loss of bladder control.

But these creatures are pussycats compared with The Tyrant, leader of the Forces of Evil and holder of the title *Most Foul, Wicked, and Depraved Being in the Galaxy* (as voted for ten Gala-years running by all other foul, wicked, and depraved beings in the Galaxy, who should know what they're talking about).

The Big Bug, leader of the Bugs, was standing in total darkness and in total fear. It had been summoned to the Dark Pyramid, the secret headquarters and main fortress of The Tyrant. The Big Bug had teleported from the prison planet of Kazamblam, thus avoiding the vast array of defenses that protected the Dark Pyramid from any being stupid enough to want to attack the mighty and assault-proof construction.

Being summoned before The Tyrant was bad. It was worse than bad. Much worse. Many of the Big Bug's predecessors had been summoned by The Tyrant. They hadn't returned, and soon after their visit, their position had been prominently advertised as an employment opportunity in magazines featuring big energy weapons on the cover and short words inside. This unnerving fact was preying on the Bug's mind as it stood in the darkness.

A blinding light exploded, illuminating the surroundings with the brilliant radiance of a thousand stars.

The startled Bug blinked, trying to take in

its surroundings. When it had done so, it whimpered.

It was standing in a huge cavern on the edge of a mighty precipice that disappeared downward into utter blackness. A thin metal bridge spanned the colossal chasm. It shimmered silvery-blue against the blackness of the drop.

Stepping back, the Bug peered across the abyss. It could just make out the dark outline of a figure silhouetted against the array of lights. The Tyrant took every precaution to conceal his identity, even from his most senior officers.

The Tyrant's voice boomed out, echoing from every wall. "You are standing on the edge of the Bottomless Abyss of Unspeakable Oblivion. Both literally and metaphorically," he added.

Although the Bug didn't understand the exact meaning of "literally and metaphorically," the implication was clear enough. Its armpits began to dampen.

"Of course, the abyss isn't *really* bottomless," continued The Tyrant, "although it *is* awfully deep. If you should fall into it, you would eventually find yourself in an ice-cold sea. Can you swim?"

The Bug shook its huge gray head.

"Not to worry. You wouldn't drown."

The Bug gave a sigh of relief.

"Because the sea is home to thousands of flesh-ripping piranha squid from the planet Aaaaaargh! They're the sea-dwelling cousins of the eyeball-popping razor-toothed ear-drillers, by the way, and their existence explains why the eyeball-popping razor-toothed ear-drillers have never learned to swim. But perhaps you're not interested in zoology."

The Bug began to sweat harder.

"Interesting creatures," continued The Tyrant. "In a matter of seconds, they can strip the flesh off a fully grown nawgaw." The Evil Lord of the FOEs paused pointedly. "Or a Bug," he added playfully.

The Bug began to sweat even more.

"What did your mother and father call you?"

A shadow of confusion crossed over the Bug's gray, horned features. What was The Tyrant getting at? The question was ridiculous — Bugs weren't born. They were the result of a genetic experiment that crossed an Antarean rhinoceros with a Lalandian hyena.

"Everyone should have a name," continued The Tyrant. "What about Eric? That's a good name. A solid name. A . . . dependable and reliable name."

"As Your Appalling Majesty wishes," replied Eric.

"Good. Now, Eric, this is what we are going to do. You are going to walk across this bridge. I will ask you a question. You will reply. If it is a question to which you can honestly answer yes, you may take one step forward. If your answer is negative, you will take two steps back. The object of the exercise is to reach this side of the abyss."

"And if I don't?"

In the silence that followed, the Bug swore it could make out the lapping of water far below.

"So," The Tyrant began. "Eric. You are leader of the Bugs, chief enforcers of my Forces of Evil?"

"Yes," answered the Big Bug.

"There, wasn't that easy? And that is not a

question!" warned The Tyrant before the Bug could answer. "Take one step forward."

The Bug complied, stepping out onto the thin metal that separated it from the terrifying drop.

"You are feared throughout the Galaxy?"

"Yes."

Another step.

"There is an unending supply of Bugs?"

"Yes."

Another step.

"Therefore you are expendable?"

There was a slight tremor in the Bug's reply. "Er — yes."

"Good. Take another step forward."

A further series of satisfactory answers brought the Bug to the middle of the bridge.

An electronic hum sounded behind the Bug. Startled, the creature turned. The part of the bridge it had walked over was retracting into the shimmering metal wall. The Tyrant's voice was cold and measured. "To help focus your mind," he explained.

The Bug gulped. The only way now was forward — or down.

"I seem to recall," said The Tyrant, "that

you promised to capture the last remaining server in Friends hands, so that I may take complete control of the Outernet. Correct?"

"Yes."

The Bug took a step forward, away from the terrifying drop.

"Not only that, you promised to capture The Weaver, the leader of the Friends."

"Yes."

Another step forward. Another step nearer to safety.

"Have you?" The Tyrant spat out the question.

"No," the Bug's voice was almost a whisper.

"Take two steps back."

The Bug did as it was ordered. Its heels hung over the edge of the thin metal. It stood, eyes closed, waiting for the inevitable, final question.

Something began to play a whiny electronic version of Dr. C. Rappers' hit single, "Baybee, I Wanna Feel Your Tentacles Round Me All Night Long." The Tyrant gave an exasperated sigh.

"What now? Interruptions, interruptions."

The Dark Lord flicked a switch and waved vaguely at the Bug. "Excuse me a moment while I take this call."

The head of Tracer, the FOEs chief surveillance officer, appeared on a bank of screens on The Tyrant's communications console. The six-armed being's elephant ears drooped in a dispirited sort of way, and his VR visor, usually pulsing with light, was dark and lifeless.

"Tracer. How good of you to get in touch. Where are you? No, don't bother answering." The Tyrant checked a set of coordinates. "I see, a trading post in the Trojan Sector."

A bead of sweat broke out on Tracer's brow. He wiped it away with two of his six claws.

"I was just discussing your latest failure with my head of security." The Tyrant's voice was as cold as the sea at the bottom of the abyss. "I understand that you traveled to a planet called Helios and took The Server from the three humans, namely Jack Armstrong, Merle Stone, and Lothar Gelt — and their renegade chameleoid companions."

"Yes, Your Gracious Evilness," replied Tracer.

"Yet you did not return it to me. I wonder why that is."

Tracer remained silent.

"Perhaps you wanted it for yourself? Perhaps you see yourself as a Dark Lord? Although since your visor is obviously not functioning, it would appear that you no longer *see* anything."

"It is as you say, Malign Majesty."

"I have *interviewed*," said The Tyrant with emphasis, "the surviving Bugs that accompanied you to Helios. They informed me (between pleas for mercy) that once you had let The Server slip from your grasping claws and lost track of it — along with the humans and their Friends — you stole an escape pod from their ship and disappeared." The Tyrant paused for effect. "However, you will be delighted to know that The Server has turned up again."

Tracer looked up suddenly.

The Tyrant chuckled softly. "I thought that might surprise you."

"Where is it, O Vexatious One?"

The Tyrant ignored the question. "Frankly, I am disappointed in you."

Tracer nodded furiously. "And because of

that I wish to tender my resignation, Your Most Deplorable Wickedness."

"The job I gave you was for life. Or in your case, death."

Tracer's thin lips twitched. "I suppose a reference is out of the question?"

"I promise you a very generous severance." The Tyrant's voice sent a chill through both of Tracer's complex spines. "I shall sever you generously for this act of betrayal. Hear this, you miserable creature. You can run from me and hide in the most remote and farthest outreaches of the Galaxy, but I will find you." The Tyrant spat out the words. "Our paths will cross again, and when they do —"

The Tyrant flicked a button. The screen went blank. The Dread Lord gave a theatrical sigh. "Now, where was I? Ah, yes. The Server . . ." The Tyrant turned his attention back to the Bug still standing on the bridge.

"We can get The Server back," babbled the Big Bug.

"Promises, promises." The Tyrant shook his head. "You are not going to have the opportunity. I will no longer tolerate your species' incompetence. I am suspending all

Bug operations forthwith and sending all Bug agents into exile. All will return to the cloning moon of Nerdoofo, until further notice." The Tyrant's voice was as hard as boron. "I will not accept failure. Failure is not an option."

"Exile!" cried the Big Bug. "But that is not fair!"

"*Fair* is a word not in my dictionary — it is far too close to *failure*."

The Big Bug stood still, the gaping abyss yawning down either side of it. "What do I do now?" it demanded bitterly, gesturing at the bridge.

"Nothing," replied the Tyrant. "This interview is over. Thank you for dropping in."

The Tyrant hit a button on his console. The bridge tilted. For a second the Big Bug tried to balance on the thin metal, arms flailing like a scarecrow in a hurricane.

Then it dropped, screaming, into the abyss.

The scream lasted a very long time. It was followed by a faint splash and more — very faint but enthusiastic — screaming.

There was silence.

The Tyrant turned back to his console and activated a hyperlink communication channel.

"Are the humans still on the planet Earth?"

"Yes." The slim figure who answered the call had green skin and hair. "And the two chameleoids. I am monitoring their movements. Do you wish me to take The Server from them?"

"If you can." The Tyrant's voice was noncommittal. "I have offered a reward for any being who brings me The Server. Even as we speak, several bounty hunters are heading for Earth by ship or teleportation, each hoping to claim the prize."

The caller gave an angry hiss. "But I am here already. I can get The Server. Don't you trust me?"

"I trust no one," The Tyrant said sharply. "I did not become the Dark Lord of the Galaxy by trusting other beings!"

The caller snorted. "Yet it seems you would entrust this mission to the most degenerate scum in the Galaxy."

"It takes one to know one," The Tyrant said mildly. "The more hunters there are, the more likely the success of the mission. If you wish to bring me The Server, then you may take your chance with everyone else."

The figure gave an angry nod. "What about the humans?"

The Evil Lord of the Galaxy didn't hesitate with his reply. "Eliminate them."

CHAPTER ONE

U.S. Air Force Base, Little Slaughter, near Cambridge, England

"Kidnapped by aliens." The policeman stared at Jack. Then he flipped his notebook shut and folded his arms across it. "You'll have to do better than that, son."

"That's not what I said." Jack shook his head wearily. "You're not listening."

"Oh, Jack!" Jack's mother was perched on the edge of the uncomfortable government-issue chair she had been offered at the start of the interview. "Tell the truth, love. Please. Then we can go home." Jack's father sat next to her, looking at the floor in moody silence.

"Let's start again at the beginning." The policeman reopened his notebook and cast a sideways glance to check that the red light of the recording machine was still on. He was not a happy man. He wasn't happy to be on the

United States Air Force base, in an unfamiliar interview room. He wasn't happy that his interview technique was being watched (and no doubt assessed) by Air Force security. He wasn't happy that Jack Armstrong had reappeared on the base instead of at his home, starting all these procedural headaches. Above all, he wasn't happy that Jack, having disappeared ten days before with two Air Force dependents (one the daughter of the base commander), wasn't telling a story that made any sense at all.

Jack spread his hands on the bare tabletop. "I've already told you. We had to leave Earth to protect The Server."

"This is the laptop computer," the policeman said stiffly, "that you say gets you on to the Galaxy-wide web and sends you to lots of alien planets."

"By teleportation, right!" Jack brightened. Maybe the policeman was starting to listen to him after all.

"Including one where you turned into a bear and your friend Merle Stone turned into a cat."

"No, you've got that wrong," said Jack helpfully. "Merle turned into a flying seal.

Googie was a cat to start with, and she turned into a gazelle, but then she turned back into a cat again."

"Of course she did. I saw her myself an hour ago, she was definitely a cat then." The policeman gazed at Jack poker-faced. "And all this was to stop your computer from falling into the hands of your enemies, the FOEs."

"Those that *have* hands, yes." Jack shuddered.

"And then you got sent back into the past, so you could tell some alien how to get this whole galactic web thing started — even though it had to exist in order to send you back to start it."

"Er — yes." Jack was a bit unclear on that part himself.

"And now you've come back to Earth to wait for some alien to contact you with instructions on how to get this computer — The Server — to the leader of the Friends, called . . ." — the policemen consulted his notes — "The Weaver?"

"You've got it." Jack nodded eagerly. His mother groaned softly.

The policeman rubbed one hand over his

face. Either the kid was lying his socks off to cover up who knew what, or this was a job for the psychiatrists. He leaned forward. "Look, son, I hope you realize the seriousness of your situation."

As the policeman reeled off the consequences of continuing to give a false account of his absence, an air base security sergeant watched Jack with narrowed eyes. The kid's story had to be a pile of baloney — except that there had been those reports of a two-headed Alien Life-Form on the base, and then Colonel Stone had started acting strange, and those two CIA men had shown up, except when they'd checked with the CIA they'd never heard of them. The sergeant wasn't an over-imaginative type, but there had been enough weird things happening at the base to make him wonder.

Some distance from the base police station, Merle was getting the third degree from her father.

She had expected Colonel Stone to put on his toughest military manner and give her the sort of lecture he reserved for airmen who'd turned up late for duty. But the reality was worse. Colonel Stone was being Reasonable, with a capital *R*. This was like being reasonable with a small *r*, except it clearly took a lot more effort. This made Merle very uncomfortable. She would prefer it if her dad started throwing furniture.

"I've tried to do the best I could," Colonel Stone was saying. Merle bit her lip. She hated it when her dad blamed himself for not bringing her up properly since her mother had been killed in a car crash.

Colonel Stone stopped pacing the room and sat down on the edge of an armchair. This put him face-to-face with Merle, who was curled up on the sofa, nervously twirling her braided hair and hugging a throw pillow. He looked directly into her eyes. Merle squirmed. Uh-oh. She was in for a man-to-man talking-to.

"I know exactly what's going on." Colonel Stone's voice was firm and measured. "You can't fool me." He began to tick off points on his fingers. "Strange computers that can send people to different planets. Two-headed aliens running around the base. Creatures that can change their shape in the blink of an eye. Time travel. Parallel realities." He paused, then said very quietly, "C'mon, Merle, you can tell me the truth, and then we can start to work this thing out." He reached out and took her hand. "It's drugs, isn't it?"

"Dad!!!"

Merle's outraged protest sent Colonel Stone pacing around the room. "Well, what is it? Will you talk to me, for Pete's sake?"

Merle gazed at him, feeling amused, resentful, and stricken with guilt at the same time. How could he think — but then, the truth *was* kinda wild. Merle sighed. How could she square things with her dad when the true story of where she'd been was one that he couldn't possibly believe? She wondered how the others were getting along — Jack, and Loaf, and Bitz.

The small brown-and-white mongrel with the lopsided ear stared at the mess of cereal and unidentifiable gristlelike tubes in his food bowl and felt his stomach turn. All around him, genuine dogs were wolfing down the disgusting stuff that humans seemed to think dogs loved (and then they had the nerve to complain about how bad dogs' breath smelled. Sheesh!). Well, maybe real dogs *did* like this junk. The problem was, Bitz wasn't a real dog. He was a chameleoid — a shape-shifting Alien Life-Form. As Friends agent Sirius, he'd had to get used to the feeding habits of the bodies that he'd assumed, some of which had been pretty bizarre. For one assignment, he'd taken on the form of a Marman megaphant beetle, living on the dung of the Marman megaphant (Bitz winced at the memory) — but even then, the megaphants hadn't manufactured the dung deliberately in the belief that the beetles *liked* it.

Bitz gave a low whine. Soon, dinnertime would be over, and then the other dogs in the pound would go back to growling, yapping, running around in circles for no particular reason, and play fighting — at least he assumed that's what it was, though his left ear still ached from a scrap with an overenthusiastic fox terrier. Bitz actually enjoyed being a dog most of the time, but that was when he was around The Server, whose translation programs allowed him to communicate with humans. Humans were pretty dumb sometimes, but at least they could hold up their end of a conversation. The longest exchange of ideas Bitz had had since coming to the pound had been:

Woof!

Woof?

Growl!

Whine?

Snarl!

As Bitz sat lost in gloom, a nearby voice said *Meow.*

Meow? That wasn't something you heard a lot in the dog pound.

Bitz casually looked around, then sidled nonchalantly over to the wire fence surrounding his prison. Googie sat primly on her haunches outside the fence. As Bitz edged closer, the cat-shaped chameleoid licked an elegant paw and smoothed down her ear. "Well, well," she said in the language of Kippo VI, her homeworld. "How are you? Having a nice time with all the other dumb mutts?"

Bitz was too depressed to give the cat an argument. "Humans!" he whined in Kippan accented with the nasal twang of Usnan, the language of his own planet in the Epsilon Sector. "We save the Galaxy, and what do they do? Lock me up in this place! I could tell you stories — there's this Doberman." Bitz shivered, then glared at Googie. "Hey! How come you get to roam around like you own the place while I'm cooped up here in the slammer?"

"It's perfectly simple," drawled Googie. "I am an independent-minded, self-willed, free-spirited cat, while you are an untrustworthy, car-chasing, sidewalk-fouling, pants-sniffing, ankle-biting, hydrant-peeing, uncivilized brute of a dog. That's why!"

Bitz bared his teeth. "Is zat so?" He turned his head and gave a yap. Heads emerged from dinner bowls. Tails went up. A cat!

Half a second later, the wire fence was thrumming from an assault of scrabbling claws. Snarling muzzles were drawn back over snapping teeth as dogs of all shapes and sizes tore at the wire to get at Googie. The cat sat washing herself, secure in the knowledge that the worst the dogs could do was make her eardrums ache.

She rose to her feet. "See you around," she told Bitz. "When you come up for parole,

24

maybe. I'm glad to see you among companions of your own intellectual level." With that, she swaggered off, deliberately staying close to the wire but just out of reach. The dogs in the pound kept pace with her, still throwing themselves at the wire in a useless, snarling frenzy.

Bitz sighed. Maybe he should have been a bit more diplomatic. He hadn't asked Googie how the humans were doing or what had happened to The Server.

Groof!

Bitz felt several drops of slobber land on his shoulder. He looked up into the grinning muzzle of a large Doberman.

Bitz's ears drooped. "Oh, brother!" he muttered to himself.

Space Trading Post 478, Trojan Sector

Halfway across the Galaxy, a droop-shouldered figure sat on a cracked plastic stool in a seedy spacer bar, wondering how long he could spin out drinking an already cold cup of Cassiopeian cappuccino before the hard-eyed proprietor threw him out. Zodiac Hobo was down on his luck and a long way from home.

The bottom had fallen out of the space-desperado business. Nobody seemed to want any illegal cargoes running these days, and there wasn't a merchant in the Galaxy dumb enough to trust Zodiac with the legal sort. Seeing the bartender swivel a suspicious antenna-top eyeball in his direction, Zodiac quickly took a sip of mud-flavored froth and wiped his green beard with a six-fingered hand that was even grubbier than usual. His beloved solar flares were covered with food stains, his space boots were down-at-the-heel, and a colony of Muscan munching moths had reduced the frills on his shirt to ribbons.

The bar where Zodiac sat feeling sorry for himself was on the worst habitat level of Space Trading Post 478 in the Trojan Sector. Zodiac was sitting there, drinking endless cups of terrible coffee, because he had nowhere else to go. He had been forced to dock at the station when the engines of his ship, *Trigger*, had started producing dense clouds of blue smoke. When he asked his ship's brain what the problem was, he immediately wished he hadn't.

"What's the problem? What's the problem?" *Trigger* had immediately spat out a string of tearful reproaches. "What do you expect? You buy cheap fuel, you never do any maintenance checks, you just take me for granted."

With *Trigger*'s complaints ringing in his ears, Zodiac had brought his ship limping in to the station at whoosh factor one, only to have his vessel locked up for previous unpaid docking fees.

The bartender writhed over to Zodiac's table on its numerous flagella, which undulated beneath it like the swirling bristles in a car wash. The green-skinned being wiped Zodiac's table with a filthy cloth, arranging the dirt into streaks. Zodiac looked up with a guilty start. "Yeah — hey, dude, this is great coffee, y'know? Like, you gotta drink it slow to get the full flavor."

"Can it, creep." As far as the bartender was concerned, customer service was something that happened to other life-forms. "There's somebody wants to see ya."

Elephant ears unfolded on either side of the bartender's back. Their owner emerged from behind his guide, and after a moment's sightless fumbling put a hand on Zodiac's shoulder. And then another hand. And then another four.

"Zodiac Hobo," hissed Tracer, The Tyrant's previously all-seeing chief of surveillance.

Zodiac's orange skin turned an unhealthy shade of yellow. "Oh, man!" he groaned. "I told you on Helios, I don't want to get involved in no heavy scene. Like, why d'you want to come here buggin' me?"

"Shut up." Two of Tracer's claws produced a small wad of notes with which he tipped the bartender, who moved away after a final unpleasant leer at Zodiac. Tracer transferred another two hands to Zodiac's collar. He twisted it in a grip of surprising strength as he slid onto the seat next to Zodiac.

Tracer's skin was still blistered from the burst of plasma energy he had suffered on the planet Helios in his attempt to break the connection between The Server and the great semiorganic computer, Tiresias. Zodiac stared at the burned-out visor on Tracer's head, which he had last seen pulsing with light as it fed information to the surveillance chief. Zodiac waved a hand in front of it. "Hooo, dude, what happened to the old peek-a-roonie? Looks like you can't even get cable on this thing."

Tracer's grip tightened. Zodiac sputtered into silence. "Spare me your foolishness," rasped the elephant-eared being. As Zodiac gasped for breath, Tracer relaxed and his rat-trap mouth curled into a sneer. "From what I hear, you're not doing so well yourself."

Zodiac massaged his throat. "Hey, man, you know how it goes," he squeaked, trying to sound nonchalant. "You win some, you lose some."

"It sounds to me as if you've been losing most of them lately." Tracer gave Zodiac his shoulder back. "Do you want a job?"

Zodiac groaned. "No way, dude. Like, I don't do government contracts, you know that."

"For reasons that do not concern you," Tracer interrupted him, "at the moment, I am on what you might call 'detached duty.'"

Zodiac's multicolored eyes narrowed shrewdly. "Had a bust up with the Big Guy, eh? Taking it on the lam?"

Tracer ignored the interruption. "I have your ship," he said casually. "I bought it this morning. I could find another pilot and put into effect the one hundred and forty-six arrest warrants that remain outstanding against your name."

Zodiac closed his eyes. "Or?" he said tone-lessly.

"Or I could have your ship repaired, and you can have it back and be free to go anywhere in the Galaxy you want." Tracer's voice became a harsh growl. "Provided it's Earth."

"You want to go to Earth?" Zodiac stirred unhappily on his stool. "Oh, man, I'm getting a bad vibe about this."

U.S. Air Force Base, Little Slaughter, near Cambridge, England

In the living room of a house on the U.S. Air Force base, Loaf was facing a drooling, red-faced creature whose throbbing purple veins stood out above bloodshot eyes that bulged almost out of its head. It wasn't much of a comfort to Loaf that the creature in question was his father.

"I got my credit card bill yesterday." Master Sergeant Gelt's voice had the rasping quality of a badly oiled chainsaw. "It seems I owe fifty billion U.S. dollars to some loan-shark company I've never heard of. I don't suppose you'd happen to know anything about this?"

Fortunately for Loaf, at that moment all the windows blew in.

CHAPTER TWO

Sirens wailed. Every street on the air base was filled with running figures — officers and airmen heading for their duty stations, their families rushing for cover. Frank Stone, struggling into a bullet-proof vest, wrenched open the front door of his house and hit the lawn running just as a jeep skidded to a halt outside. The colonel vaulted into the passenger seat and turned to glare at Merle as she hopped in back. "Where d'you think you're going?"

Merle glared right back at him. "I'm coming to Operations with you."

"You're going to the shelter!"

Merle shook her head. "You need me. The book doesn't cover what's happening here." She pointed at the sky. "Have you seen what's bombing us?"

Frank Stone followed his daughter's finger — and gaped.

Overhead, a spacecraft that looked like a silver running shoe tore across the sky. It was followed by something that looked like a flying steam iron with torpedo-shaped outriggers. Both ships fired energy weapons at something out of sight behind the base houses. Whatever they hit went *crump*. There was a lot of smoke.

"What on Earth?" Her father turned an incredulous face to Merle. "No. Cancel that. Nothing *on Earth*. Friends of yours?"

Merle shook her head. "Far from it. This is a close encounter of the fourth kind."

Her father stared. "The fourth kind?"

Merle ducked as a horseshoe-shaped craft powered overhead. "Yeah — that's where the aliens shoot at you."

Colonel Stone hitched up his jaw. "Okay. You're with me. There's a steel helmet under your seat. Put it on."

The jeep set off with a squeal of rubber. Merle found the helmet and made a face. It weighed a ton. It would *destroy* her hair.

Something like a flying motorcycle shot

overhead. The road in front of them exploded. The jeep swerved violently. Merle put the helmet on.

Across the base, Loaf grabbed desperately at the door handle of his dad's motor home.

"Siddown," snarled Master Sergeant Gelt, hauling at the wheel of the cumbersome vehicle to turn it violently around a crater.

"Dad!" Loaf's face was white with fear. "Shouldn't we be heading for the shelter? I mean, it's *dangerous* out here. What are you doing?"

"Protecting my investment!"

"What investment? Dad, you can't be serious! I know you're into wheeling and dealing in a big way, but it's Air Force property the aliens are destroying. All these airplanes and trucks and stuff belong to the U.S. government — they don't belong to you!"

The master sergeant glared at his son. "Wanna bet?"

Before Loaf could reply, a movement in the rearview mirror caught his eye. He screamed like a cat with its tail caught in a slamming door.

Something that looked like a flying gyroscope zeroed in on the outsized camper. There was a flash of light, and the body of the monstrous vehicle exploded into shards of composition board, aluminium sheeting, and tasteless upholstery.

Now driving little more than a flatbed truck with no back to its cab, Master Sergeant Gelt cast a livid look at his gibbering son. "That's coming out of *your* allowance!"

Bitz ran toward the hole in the fence where a speeding car, its driver distracted by a horseshoe-shaped alien spacecraft crossing the road in front of it, had powered straight through. Behind him, a whimpering Doberman was trying to hide underneath an upturned cage. Bitz reached the hole. He paused. He went back into the pound and bit the Doberman savagely on the leg.

Then he headed for the center of the excitement as fast as his short legs could carry him.

"Look, Sergeant! I have to get to Colonel Stone."

Jack was finding it difficult to stay calm.

Apart from the bombardment, his mother and father were trying to pull him down to the floor, into the questionable shelter of the interview room table.

The sergeant, holding his sidearm as if not quite sure what to do with it, turned from the window. "This is a combat situation, mister! There's nothing in the rule book that says suspects in detention get to see the commanding officer."

"Is there anything in the rules about what to do if the base is attacked by alien spacecraft?"

The sergeant frowned. The kid had a point. On the other hand, if he let a suspect out of custody without authorization, he'd probably be demoted to airman third class in charge of latrines.

Movement outside the window caught his eye. A nine-foot reptilian alien wearing bronze armor was striding toward the detention block. It carried what was clearly an energy weapon the size of a small truck. The sergeant swung around. "On the floor," he snapped. "Cover your heads."

The policeman, who had been trying without success to contact his inspector by cell phone for further instructions, glared at the security man. "Don't give me orders," he said tightly. "I'm a member of the British police."

"Good for you." The sergeant jerked his head toward the window. "Why don't you arrest *him*?"

The policeman said nothing. He reached inside his jacket and pulled out a small leather wallet. Then, before the sergeant's unbelieving gaze, he squared his shoulders and marched out the door.

Standing on the steps of the detention block, the policeman held his badge like a very inadequate shield and said in a ringing voice, "I'm arresting you on charges of affray, causing a public nuisance, and willful damage to property. You're not obliged to say anything, but . . ."

Recovering from his astonishment, the sergeant shoulder-charged the policeman to the ground and dropped into a firing stance. He emptied a full clip of ammunition at the alien.

Some invisible force field around the alien sparkled. Bullet shells dropped harmlessly to the road. The sergeant gulped. The alien gave him a wicked grin and raised its weapon.

The sergeant dived to one side just in time.

When he had recovered sufficiently from the near miss, the sergeant staggered to his feet, turned — and let out a hollow groan.

His prisoner and his prisoner's parents had disappeared.

So had the detention block.

"What's the story, Hal?"

Colonel Stone strode into the operations room with Merle at his heels. Major Hal Jackson, the colonel's aide, wasted no time questioning her arrival.

"There are at least a dozen vessels attacking us," he said crisply. "Maybe more. They're moving so fast it's hard to keep count. There seem to be other attackers using some kind of jet packs or antigravity devices, flycycles . . ." Jackson's voice rose as he shrugged helplessly. "We don't even have *words* for the hardware these guys are using."

Colonel Stone was staring at the status board. "Defenses?"

The major regained his composure. "We

had time to scramble a couple of F15s, but they were downed after they reported complete systems failure. Pilots ejected. The other birds' engines won't even fire up. We managed to get off some surface-to-air missiles, but they exploded well before reaching their targets. So now we're down to semiautomatic weapons and rock throwing."

"Have we informed U.S.A.F.E. H.Q.? The Pentagon?"

Jackson shook his head. "We have a complete communications blackout. Radio, all frequencies; landlines, computers, cell and satellite phones — everything's down."

"Dad." Merle's voice was calm but insistent. "You know who they're after — and what."

Colonel Stone said nothing. Locked in the most secure safe the base could provide, along with some very important keys and envelopes containing instructions and codes that Colonel Stone didn't even want to think about, was an ordinary-looking (more or less) laptop computer. The colonel hadn't bought Merle's story that this device was in truth a staggeringly sophisticated alien communications device called The Server, but he hadn't reached command rank in the world's largest air force by taking unnecessary risks.

"Merle!" A wild-eyed boy of Merle's age had ducked past the MPs guarding the door and now had her by the arms, shaking her. "These aliens are after The Server. If they don't get it, they'll wreck the base. We could get seriously killed!"

The MPs caught up with Loaf and dragged him away from Merle just as Master Sergeant Carl Gelt appeared, gasping for breath and smoldering slightly. He gave a sketchy salute. "Reporting for duty, sir!"

"At ease, Sergeant." Colonel Stone gave Loaf an unfriendly glance. "Restrain your son. Sit on him if necessary."

"I'm afraid Loaf's right, sir."

Colonel Stone's face grew livid as he glared at the sloppily dressed kid and his nervous-looking parents, who must have come in while the MPs' attention was on Loaf. As a Brit — and a civilian — and a minor, Jack Armstrong had absolutely no business at all in Ops, but he carried himself with an air of quiet author-ity that suggested he did.

"Colonel," Jack continued, "the aliens are here for The Server — and probably for me, Merle, and Loaf as well." His mother put a protective hand on Jack's shoulder, which he gently removed. "We've been telling you the truth, Colonel. I don't blame you for not believing us, but right now the truth really *is* out there, and the FOEs will go on tearing your base apart just as long as they know we're here."

The colonel was tempted, based on his training and everything he believed, to make a stinging response. Instead, he proved that he was worth his exalted rank by saying, "What do you suggest?"

Space Trading Post 478, Trojan Sector

The Cyclopian customs and immigration officer looked up from the deskful of forms it was filling out with infuriating slowness and gave Zodiac Hobo an unfriendly look. Zodiac wasn't fazed by this. Cyclopians gave *everyone* unfriendly looks.

The Cyclopian transferred the intimidating gaze of its single unblinking eye onto Zodiac's suitcase. It was a large, cheap, polyester-type model, and from the way Zodiac was struggling with it, obviously very heavy.

Zodiac put the bag down (the Cyclopian wondered for a moment whether he could possibly have heard a muffled *ooof!* from inside) and slapped a semitransparent plastic folder down on the desk in front of the intimidating official. "Release form," he said cheerfully. "Filled in and signed in octuplicate. This certifies that I've paid all outstanding fees and am free to leave this facility." He grinned at the charmless official. "Like, parting is such sweet sorrow, dude."

The Cyclopian gave a disappointed grunt on general principles and checked the form with maddening slowness. Eventually, it reluctantly conceded that everything seemed to be in order and Zodiac was free to go.

Zodiac produced another form. "Clearance application for passage to Earth, dude."

"Earth?" The Cyclopian narrowed its eye suspiciously. "Why Earth?"

Zodiac gave a careless shrug. "I hear The Tyrant is looking for bounty hunters for a short but well-paid assignment. Like, I've decided to try my luck."

The Cyclopian gave Zodiac a contemptuous look. "You don't look like a bounty hunter to me."

"Better believe it, dude." Zodiac gave the Cyclopian an outrageous wink. "I specialize in secret missions."

The Cyclopian sniffed contemptuously. "I've never heard of you."

Zodiac gave him a big, friendly grin. "See? That's how good I am. Licensed to kill, thrill, and chill."

"I'll have to get authorization for this." The Cyclopian picked up the form and lumbered off through a door marked PRIVATE.

"Don't overdo it!" said Zodiac's suitcase in complaining tones. "I thought you were going to blow the whole deal."

Zodiac shook the case with unnecessary force. "You okay in there, man?"

"Ow! No thanks to you. And don't call me *man*!"

"Don't sweat it."

"I am not, as you so charmingly put it,

'sweating it.'" Tracer's voice was muffled. "Which is more than I can say for your socks."

Zodiac kicked the case in warning as the Cyclopian returned. "Passage approved," it grunted. Then its eye took on an unpleasant glint. "What's in the case?"

Zodiac replied cheerfully, "My underwear." He paused slightly. "Used."

The Cyclopian looked hard at Zodiac. It took in the dirty bell-bottom pants, the moth-eaten shirt, the tangled beard, and the straggly hair.

It hurriedly stamped CHECKED on the suitcase. Zodiac made his way to the embarkation lock, whistling all the way.

U.S. Air Force Base, Little Slaughter, near Cambridge, England

The Server sat on a side table of the Ops room with all the ominous innocence of an unexploded grenade.

Colonel Stone stared at it. "That's what this is all about?"

Jack nodded. "Help."

Colonel Stone drew back with a sharp in-

44

take of breath as the hologram of The Server's unreliable Help application appeared, floating in its usual place above the keyboard. "Now you want Help?! You let me be snatched by a bunch of know-nothing primates and locked in some miserable vault. Do you know how bad that is for my claustrophobia?"

"Give it a rest," Jack told it. "You're on the air force base. Who's attacking us?"

"Always the questions!" Help complained. "Lemme monitor recent o-mail announcements." After a slight pause it continued, "The Tyrant has fired the Bugs."

Merle gave a relieved whistle. "Good."

"Not good," snapped Help. "He's sicced bounty hunters on you instead. They're not as strong as Bugs, but they're twice as sneaky. And they're motivated by the most powerful force in the Galaxy."

"Money," said Loaf confidently.

"You got it."

At that moment, a scruffy mongrel dog and an aristocratic-looking cat with distinctive blue-tinged fur slid into the room.

"Hi, Jack," growled Bitz. "What's the plan?"

Googie leaped onto the table beside The Server. "Why are you all sitting around? Don't you think we should be getting out of here?"

Major Jackson gave a hollow groan. "Talking dogs and cats. Now I've seen everything!" Colonel Stone shook his head in disbelief.

The building shook as a blast from an alien weapon detonated nearby.

"Googie's right," said Merle. "The bounty hunters are after *us* and The Server, not the base. Get ready to teleport."

"But teleporting will give our position away," protested Loaf.

Merle gave him a scornful look. "I think they already *know* our position!" She bent over The Server and began to punch at the keys. "I'll try to input some coordinates."

"Where to?" said Jack.

"Anywhere other than here."

"Just a minute, young lady!" roared Colonel Stone. "You aren't going anywhere."

"Don't worry, Dad," Merle gave her father a big, winning smile. "I have my phone, so you can keep in touch, and . . ."

She was interrupted by a commotion in the corridor outside. Two MPs darted into the Operations room, slamming the heavy steel door behind them. A rhythmic electronic throbbing noise sounded from the other side of the door, which glowed bright yellow. Gleaming particles of light appeared in the middle of the door, forming a whirlpool pattern, like water swirling down a bathtub drain, with a void at its center. The vortex spread. Within seconds the door disappeared.

As the startled security men stepped back, a nightmarish alien creature, twitching violently and waving horrendous-looking weapons in all directions, slithered through the empty doorframe.

"Uh-oh." Help immediately disappeared into the relative safety of The Server. A sign appeared on its screen.

clOseD dUe to cOwaRdiCe.

"Make any sudden moves you want," screeched the intruder. It gave an insane cackle. Its four bloodshot eyes rotated crazily in different directions. "Do something stupid, and everybody'll get hurt. I'm gonna melt ya! I'm gonna melt ya!"

CHAPTER THREE

Deep Space

Zodiac jabbed at a tiny wire. "How about this?"

Zeeuuuaaaarrghhh!!! Tracer's eight limbs shot out into a dead starfish position, and his ears went rigid.

Zodiac gave a sheepish grin. "So — not that one?"

"Mr. Hobo," said Tracer through clenched teeth. "Do not do that again . . . or I will hurt you very badly."

Zodiac nodded. "I dig your lick, dude."

As *Trigger* sped through the blackness of deep space en route to Earth, Tracer had insisted that Zodiac make an attempt to fix his burned-out VR visor. This was turning out to not be one of his better decisions. Zodiac was to DIY what The Tyrant was to galactic peace and harmony.

"Very well, let us continue." Tracer wiped sweat from his brow and shook his ears. "Now, *making sure you don't touch what you touched last time*, attach the pink plasma diode to the purple wire."

Zodiac gave a low groan. "Ohhh, man. Ain't no point in talking about colors to a Jivan. We see everything in all the colors of the rainbow, all the time."

Tracer gave a deep sigh. "Judging from your fashion sense, I should have guessed."

Zodiac completed the connection. Tracer's visor fizzed and burst into fitful life. Light pulsed intermittently across the black plastic.

"Yo! Sparkly," whooped Zodiac, punching the air. "Am I the daddy or what!"

Tracer frowned. "Mr. Hobo, are you by any chance standing on your head?"

Zodiac looked puzzled. "No, dude."

"Then you've wired my visor incorrectly, you fool!" screamed Tracer. "Everything is upside down!"

Zodiac clumsily fiddled with the visor's circuitry for a few more minutes, until Tracer finally said, "Enough, it's working." He looked around, taking in the less than luxurious surroundings. "This ship can actually fly? Incredible."

Trigger sniffed. "Charming."

Tracer checked the navigation display. "But we are still several hundred light-years from Earth."

Zodiac slapped his thigh. "Bummer! Then we aren't gonna get to the party on time. All the cake will have been eaten."

"I think we will."

Zodiac shook his head. "No way, daddio. Even if we travel at whoosh factor fifty, which *Trigger* ain't close to being able to do, we'll still take years. So how you planning to get there — t-mail?"

Tracer shook his head decisively. "The Tyrant will be closely monitoring all Earthbound t-mails. The minute we try to teleport to Earth, we will be diverted to Kazamblam, or even worse, to the Dark Pyramid. We're going to take a shortcut."

"A shortcut?" Zodiac thought for a second.

Then he grinned and winked broadly at Tracer. "Like, are you thinking of taking *Trigger* through a wormhole? Haaaaaa-haaaa-haaa-ha-h . . ." Zodiac's laugh died on his lips as he caught sight of Tracer's unsmiling face. "Oh, man, you are kidding me."

Trigger gave a high-pitched wail. "Wormholes!"

"You have rocks in your head," moaned Zodiac. "Using wormholes as a form of interstellar travel is crazy dangerous."

"No, it's simple." Tracer's voice was matter-of-fact. "We steer into the mouth of a wormhole, travel through it, and emerge at the other end of the hole. Thus we cut through time and space and end up in the Sol System, very near to Earth."

"What if this mouth eats us? Come on, dude," pleaded Zodiac. "This trip sounds like one big downer. I reckon we should put this crazy idea to a vote."

"I'm against it!" said *Trigger* immediately. "Anyway, I don't want to help you chase the humans — especially the one called Merle. She was nice to me. She gave me my name.

She didn't make me go through nasty worm-holes."

"Operationally challenged ships' brains don't get a vote!" interrupted Tracer.

"Tyrant!" sniffed *Trigger*.

"Not yet," replied Tracer. He turned to Zodiac. "All organic life-forms against using a wormhole?"

Both of Zodiac's hands shot up.

"Those for." One by one, Tracer slowly raised all six of his arms. He smiled. "You're outvoted by six to two."

"Hey, no way, José. Man, that is so not fair," protested Zodiac. "Limbs are not democratic, otherwise Munervian millipedes would always get elected. Come on, Tracer dude, there's one of me and one of you."

Tracer nodded slowly. "You're right, of course. We need a tiebreaker." He reached into the depths of his jacket, pulled out a lethal-looking energy weapon, and pointed it at the space hippie's head.

Zodiac shifted uncomfortably in his seat. "Oh, man. Motion passed."

U.S. Air Force Base, Little Slaughter, near Cambridge, England

The alien bounty hunter stood framed in the hole formerly known as *door*, twitching uncontrollably. Its bright yellow skin glowed in the harsh fluorescent light of the Ops room. Glistening fangs protruded from both its slavering mouths. It was covered in leather from head to lower tentacle, with leather crossbelts and matching leather accessories.

Jack's mother gave a little scream. "It's horrible!"

"Yeah." Merle shuddered. "Leather is *soooo* passé."

"Take it out," Colonel Stone commanded harshly. But before the guards could raise their rifles, the creature fired. A blue bolt of plasma energy lit up the room, momentarily blinding everyone. The guards gasped in astonishment as their guns melted in their hands.

The being's eyes spun with evil delight. "Next time, I set it to disintegrate *you*. I'll melt ya all!"

The colonel gestured to his troops. "Take it easy, and back off."

The bounty hunter pointed several of his weapons at the companions. "Where izzz it? Where izzz it?" it hissed from one of its mouths.

Bitz padded forward. He stood between the hunter and Jack. "Where's what, ugly?"

The creature turned its maniacal eyes on the chameleoid. "Don't make me mad, don't make me mad! They don't call me Mad Moxie for nothing! If I get mad, you'll regret it."

Merle stole a quick glance at The Server. "Can't he see it?" she hissed to Jack.

"He doesn't know what it looks like," Jack whispered back. "The Server can look like anything it wants, remember?"

"I programmed the teleport." Merle breathed. "All I have to do is press SEND, but if I touch The Server he'll spot it."

Mad Moxie gave a squeal of rage. "I want The Server! Gimme, gimme, gimme!"

Bitz bared his teeth. "You don't scare us," he growled.

"Yes, it does," whimpered Loaf. "A lot."

Steam poured from Mad Moxie's three

nostrils. "You're making me mad. You won't like me when I'm mad."

Bitz snarled. "I'm not crazy about you *now*."

Jack's father stepped forward, his eyes glinting with anger. "See here, mister. I don't like your manners, and I don't like the way you come barging in here, threatening my family."

Jack gulped. His father was talking to this psychopathic alien as if he were scolding Jack for not cleaning his room.

Mad Moxie twitched even more. "Ohhhh! You just made me mad. You shouldn't have done that!" He turned several of his weapons on Jack's father. Steam shot from its nostrils, and its eyes spun uncontrollably. "I'm gonna melt ya, I'm gonna melt ya!"

BLAM!

Mad Moxie's four eyes stopped spinning. The creature looked down at the hole in its chest. "Hey, somebody's gone and melted me." It toppled over and lay still.

"Howdee."

A tall, thin humanoid with bright blue eyes blazing out of an almost translucent face stood at the doorway. It wore a simple cloth poncho draped over its shoulders. It blew at the muzzle of a smoking energy pistol and drawled, "They call me the Thing with No Name."

Jack sighed with relief. "You got here just in time, mister . . . um . . . Thing. Thank you."

"That thank you might be a little premature," rasped the creature. "I've come for The Server."

"What server?" asked Jack innocently.

The Thing's eyes narrowed to mere slits. "The Server that's translating every word you and I say. The black box that the girl is trying to hide behind her back."

Merle looked desperately toward Jack. He shrugged helplessly.

"Merle," ordered Colonel Stone, "give him The Server."

"But Dad!" protested Merle. "The future of the Galaxy . . ."

"Do it!" her father snapped.

"Glad to see someone has some sense around these parts." The Thing with No Name held out a seven-fingered hand.

"Hold it right there!" A commanding voice rang out across the Ops room.

"No more aliens," moaned Loaf. "I'm all fed up with Alien Life-Forms."

The new arrival was a female humanoid seven feet tall, with green skin and spiky hair the color and texture of grass. She wore a tight one-piece black outfit in some shiny material. She was only carrying one energy weapon, but she looked as if she knew how to use it.

"Tingkat Bumbag!" The Thing with No Name swung its energy pistol around to cover the new arrival.

Loaf snickered. "Tingkat Bumbag?"

The green-skinned woman gave Loaf a look that made the laughter die in his throat. "That's my name. Do you find it amusing?" Loaf shook his head frantically.

The Thing with No Name faced Tingkat squarely. "Sorry, Tingkat. You may be top gun hunter in the Galaxy, but according to the rules of bounty hunting, paragraph seventeen, section three-zero-eight, clause six, 'first come, first served.'"

Tingkat held up a long green finger. "But you're forgetting the number one rule."

The Thing's brow creased in puzzlement. "What's that?"

BLAM!

The Thing slumped to the floor. Tingkat lowered her gun. "Paragraph one, section one, clause one. 'The being that shoots first, wins.'" She turned to the humans. "And now, I'll have The Server, if you please."

"If we hand it over to you, what happens to us?" asked Jack, trying to stall for time.

"The Tyrant wants you," replied Tingkat, "dead or not alive."

Loaf looked puzzled. "Don't you mean dead or alive?"

Tingkat shook her head. "No, he was quite specific about that point. He's a very vindictive being. Give me The Server."

Merle and Jack exchanged glances. Merle held out The Server. As Tingkat lowered her weapon to take her prize, Merle's hand darted across The Server's keyboard and hit the SEND key. The room was filled with an explosion of blue-and-white light and noise. Then there was silence.

Every human in the Ops room stared at the

empty space that, a moment before, had held three teenagers, a cat, a dog, and a mighty powerful laptop computer. With a cry of rage, Tingkat raised her weapon, aimed it at the remaining humans, then lowered it again. "I should kill you for this insult!" she hissed. "But perhaps you will be of use later."

With that, she stepped over the bodies of the two ex-bounty hunters and stalked out, leaving Colonel Stone and his troops wide-eyed and shaking and Jack's mother and father hugging each other in relief.

Deep Space

"Is that it?" asked Zodiac, staring out of *Trigger*'s view panel at the swirling mass of energy. "That's the entrance to the wormhole?"

"Yes," replied Tracer. "And the opposite end of the hole brings us out near Earth and The Server — which will soon be mine."

Zodiac stared at the writhing hole. It seemed almost alive. "I heard that at the end of every wormhole there's a pot of enriched plutonium," he said dreamily. "Is that true?"

"No."

Zodiac gave a disappointed sigh. "Why is it called a wormhole, anyway?" he asked.

"You'll find out," replied Tracer.

Flopping back into his seat, Zodiac gulped. "Am I going to like finding out?"

"Probably not."

Zodiac gave a moan and shut his eyes tightly.

"Set coordinates," Tracer commanded.

"C-c-co-ord-d-d-inates set-t-t," stammered *Trigger*.

"Whoosh factor ten."

With a scream, *Trigger* roared into the gaping mouth of the wormhole. Zodiac's body was thrust into his seat. "Whhaaahhhh! Is this going to work?" he squealed.

Tracer's visor pulsed red. "Of course it is. Trust me."

N-space

"I'm back home!" Bitz wagged his tail in glee. "Usnan III, my home planet!"

The companions had rematerialized in a huge plastic dome with antiseptic white floors.

Clear pipes, filled with multicolored liquids, lined the walls. They looked like giant lava lamps. Bubbles formed and glooped inside the ducts. Small clouds of steam hung in the air.

Bitz breathed in deeply. "It's good to be back."

Jack shook his head. "I don't think you *are* back. Look outside."

The dome seemed to be floating in a stream of rainbow particles that flowed up, down, and around in ever-changing patterns.

"We're in N-space again," said Jack as a familiar bald-headed figure materialized before the Friends. "Hello, Janus!"

The former Friends agent regarded them solemnly with his yellow eyes. "Greetings to you all."

Bitz gave a joyful yap. "You created this setting from my mind. Thanks, Janus."

"I'm surprised he found anything at all in *your* mind," muttered Googie. Bitz gave her a hard stare.

"So this is what your planet looks like?" Jack gave Bitz a surprised look. "It's so clean! I'd never have believed you were from such a world." Jack caught Bitz's offended look. "I mean, you're . . . sort of scruffy."

"Why do you think I'm not too keen on this body I'm stuck in?" growled Bitz. "Oh, for a germ-free environment!"

Merle turned on Janus. "I didn't program The Server to bring us here! You keep doing this to us! Ever since you wound up in N-space, you drag us in here whenever you want, like we're your puppets or something."

Janus shook his head resignedly. "Merle, will you never forgive me for making you abandon Lothar?"

Merle said nothing. Their last meeting with Janus had been an unhappy one, involving time travel, parallel realities, and meeting Loaf's alternative self, a brave, heroic Lothar Gelt. On a mission to help create the Outernet, they had taken Lothar from his reality on an alternate Earth and left him behind — a hundred years in the past, on the forest planet Vered II.

"Considering your predicament," continued Janus, "this seemed to me to be an opportune moment for us to meet."

"Last time we met you," Loaf complained,

"you sent us back to Earth and told us to wait until we were contacted."

"You were," Janus pointed out.

"By a bunch of weapon-toting alien psychos!" exclaimed Loaf in exasperation.

"I did not say *who* would contact you."

Loaf shook his head. "Whoa! You are more slippery than my old man!"

Jack took The Server from Merle and held it to his chest. "Why have you brought us here again, Janus?"

"I had to," explained Janus. "The FOEs have placed a divert to send any t-mail originating on Earth straight to the deepest dungeon in The Tyrant's Dark Pyramid. Had I not intercepted your teleport, The Tyrant would already have you and The Server at his mercy."

"*Mercy*? Yeah, right," muttered Bitz. "He's got a lot of that."

"But the bounty hunters are after us!" snapped Loaf. "How are we supposed to stay ahead of them? They've got spaceships and big zappy weapon things that are going to be very bad for our health. The net is closing in on us."

Janus shook his head. "A net is just a series of holes. You can go through them. You will use teleportation to escape and keep ahead of these hunters."

Merle clenched her fists. "But you just said . . ."

Janus held up a hand. "Let me explain. There is a teleportation system on Earth that predates Outernet technology, but you have to be in the right place to use it. There are five such sites, each one on a different continent."

"Ancient sites!" Bitz tried to slap his forehead with his paw and missed. "Why didn't I think of that?"

"There are seven continents," Merle pointed out. She counted them off on her fingers. "North America, South America, Europe, Africa, Asia, Australia, and Antarctica. Seven."

"The ancients regarded the Americas as one continent," replied Janus.

"Well, that still leaves six," said Loaf.

"You are right, but the site on Antarctica has long vanished. It was called Atlantis."

Bitz nodded. "Pity about the accident."

Merle curled her lip. "Atlantis? An accident? You're kidding me."

"Humans!" said Googie. "They never could resist meddling with elemental forces."

"Nobody knows," Janus said, "whether such sites were left by technologically advanced Earth natives who have since disappeared or whether they were built by alien visitors in ancient times. Each site retains many hidden powers. One of these is the power to teleport between the sites."

"So it's just like t-mail?" asked Loaf.

Janus shook his head. "Only in the sense that riding a broomstick is like flying in an airliner."

"Draftier," added Bitz. "And a lot more risky. Plus, you don't get an in-flight movie."

Janus continued his explanation. "In each location, you must initiate the site's defenses by identifying and pressing a symbol before moving on to the next. The combined power of all the existing sites will create an ancient defense against invasion." Janus paused for a second. "They will form a kind of primitive but powerful Chain around the planet. This will evict the bounty hunters from Earth and prevent any more invaders from arriving."

"So what you're saying," said Loaf sarcastically, "is that it's up to us to save the Galaxy." He rolled his eyes theatrically. "Again."

Janus ignored the interruption. "Help will assist you in identifying the correct symbols. It has the necessary information in its data banks. Remember, after this meeting, you cannot use The Server again for teleportation until all sites have been activated. I will now send you to the first site." He made the secret sign of the Friends. "Go well."

A white vortex engulfed the companions. The glass dome was replaced with a sea of living particles. Jack once again experienced the feeling of being ripped apart atom by atom, then being smashed back together. With a final jolt, he felt whole again. He blinked, taking in the new surroundings.

"Oh, no," moaned Bitz. "Not here again."

CHAPTER FOUR

Near Saturn, Sol System

Zodiac's ship, looking pretty beaten up, shot through a hole in the black fabric of the sky.

Inside, Zodiac sat wide-eyed, his mouth opening and shutting like a large koi carp. He gave a cry that was no more than a breath. "The horror! The horror!"

Tracer rubbed his claws together. "There, now, that wasn't so bad, was it? Admittedly, some of those worms were a trifle playful, and their seventeen sets of teeth can be a little disconcerting, but all in all, I'd say it was a good trip."

"I want my motherboard!" cried *Trigger*, bursting into tears.

Ignoring the blubbering spaceship, Tracer plotted their position. Several hundred thousand miles away on *Trigger*'s starboard side was a huge planet, surrounded by three rings of icy particles, dust, and other space debris. Tracer checked its coordinates. A planet called Saturn. Good. Tracer gave a smile. He wandered over to the view panel and looked out, searching for a distant speck in the blackness. He found it. "Earth," he muttered to himself. And what was the name of the country on a small island? The answer came to him. "Ah, yes. England."

U.S. Air Force Base, Little Slaughter, near Cambridge, England

Tingkat strode across the deserted airfield toward her spaceship. What little resistance there had been to the hunters had been broken. Most of the air base personnel had already taken shelter from the alien invaders. Since the first wave of attacks, dozens of hunters had appeared. The Tyrant's message had been well and truly received, Tingkat reflected sourly. All the scum and dregs of the Galaxy had made their way to this small planet, hoping for the big payday. She had beaten them all to the prize, but The Server had slipped from her fingers. *What to do next?* she wondered.

Her wrist communicator buzzed. She flicked it open and poked at it with a long green finger.

"You do not appear to be doing very well in your mission."

Tingkat recognized the dark tones of The Tyrant, but the fact that she was thousands of light-years from the Dread Lord emboldened her. "If you hadn't sent the others . . ."

"Never question my decisions!" The voice was quiet but nonetheless threatening. "Or you will be truly sorry."

Tingkat bit her forked tongue and remained silent.

"I have news for you. I have been monitoring teleportation events in your sector. A t-mail sent from your current position has arrived at a location nearby. You must go there immediately. Seize The Server. And this time do not fail."

Tingkat's pulse raced. "Where is it?"

The Tyrant's voice was full of menace. "A place called Stonehenge."

Stonehenge, Salisbury Plain, England

The great stones of Stonehenge were silhouetted against the setting sun. The site was deserted except for the companions, who stood alone in the middle of the ruined circle of stones.

"Strange that our journey should begin here," said Bitz, "considering this was where Janus and I arrived on Earth." He looked up at Jack, who had said nothing since their arrival. "Hey, Jack! You paying attention?"

Jack shook his head slowly. "Did you see how my dad stood up to that crazy alien? I never knew he had it in him."

"Jumping june bugs! Snap out of it!" yapped Bitz. "We have to find the symbols to activate this site and teleport to the next one."

Jack nodded and held out The Server. "Janus said we should ask Help."

Ching!

The hologram appeared. "Have all those alien head bangers gone?" it asked, taking in the landscape. It did a double take. "Oh, no! We're not here again!"

"Yes, they have," said Bitz. "And yes, we are."

"So what's cooking?"

Jack quickly explained the problem. "Janus said you would have something on ancient sites in your data banks."

Help looked pained. "Something? *Something?* I have more knowledge in my least important processor than whole planetary systems put together, and you thought I might have *something* in my data banks. Sheesh!"

"Then you can tell us how this site should be activated?"

"Work, work, work, work, work," moaned Help. "How you monkeys ever became self-sufficient, I'll never know."

"Look it up in your data banks," Merle said sweetly.

"Suddenly, everyone's an expert," replied Help. It briefly disappeared back into The Server before reemerging with a smile on its hologrammatic face. "Okay, here's *something* I know. When the sun sets or rises, its light reveals symbols on the stones. Push the right

one, and hey, press-to! (That's a gag, if anyone's listening.) You activate the site."

Loaf gave a disparaging snort. "Oh, come
on! That sort of stuff is so Hollywood. You're
joking, right?"

Help materialized itself a big cigar and
a boot-polish mustache. "I say, I say, I say,
what's the difference between an ameba and
the monkey that made that last comment? The
ameba has more brains!" The hologram
glared at Loaf. "*That* was a joke — the information I gave you wasn't." Help disappeared
back into The Server, with an angry *ching*!

"Nice going, Loaf," said Merle. "Upsetting
our information source."

"But that's crazy!" protested Loaf. "You
have to wait for the sun to rise or set? What if
it's raining?"

"That's the problem with these low-tech
sites," said Bitz. "Unreliable."

"Luckily, the sun hasn't set yet," said Jack.
"Let's spread out and keep our eyes peeled for
any symbols."

As the sun dipped lower and lower in the
sky, the group fanned out across the circle,
searching for the signs that would help them

activate the site. Stonehenge was bathed in the embers of the dying day, but there was nothing to be found.

Finally, the sun disappeared from the evening sky, and darkness enveloped the ancient monument.

The companions gathered together by one of the great stones.

Loaf gave a shrug. "So the Hollywood bit didn't work. What do we do now?"

Jack shook his head. "I don't know."

U.S. Air Force Base, Little Slaughter, near Cambridge, England

"Have we managed to reestablish contact with the outside world?" asked Colonel Stone.

Major Jackson shook his head. "Still complete communication blackout. No one knows what's been happening here."

Colonel Stone grimaced. "Let me know as soon as we have a phone working. I have to contact Merle."

The colonel did not know what to make of the past few days. His daughter had been missing and then turned up again with some crazy story about aliens that he didn't believe for one minute until things with tentacles and more than the regulation number of heads had started appearing like wasps around a picnic. Then Merle and her friends disappeared before his very eyes, and to top it all off, there were a couple of dead aliens in his Ops room. *The X-Files* had nothing on this. How was it all going to sound in a report?

"The base is clear," said the major. "The Bug-Eyed Monsters seem to have disappeared. We have the situation under control."

"You think so?" Frank Stone's voice was bitter. "My kid's out there, Hal. Facing who knows what."

"Colonel." The voice at his shoulder was that of Bill Armstrong. "She's with my son. He's got his head screwed on, our Jack." He gave a slight nod. "I'll take my wife home now, if you don't mind. You'll let us know if you hear anything?" Colonel Stone nodded.

Luckily for his peace of mind, he didn't know the reason the invaders had abandoned their attack — because they had seen Tingkat leaving the base in pursuit of Merle and her friends. Among the Galaxy's bounty hunters,

74

Tingkat had a reputation for finding her prey, so the surviving hunters were pursuing her in spaceships, flycycles, jet packs, and anything else they could get ahold of that would allow them to move quickly enough.

"Major, get me reports on how many of our birds are down and an update on the state of our missile defense capabilities," Colonel Stone ordered. He stared down at the bodies of Mad Moxie and the Thing with No Name. "And, Hal, get those two creatures out of my Ops room."

"Sergeant Master Gelt volunteered to do it. He's on the case as we speak."

"You mean he's gonna try and sell 'em to some film director!" Colonel Stone gave a bark of savage laughter, not knowing how near the truth he was. "Keep the base on a state of red alert. If any more of those alien creatures appear, give it to 'em good."

Unfortunately for Tracer and Zodiac Hobo, the next alien ship to appear over the air force base was *Trigger*.

Zodiac was still shaking from the encounter with the wormhole. "They were all wormy, man. Wriggly with teeth! I haven't had a trip like that since I mistook some Andalesian funny juice for a glass of water!"

"Please be quiet, Mr. Hobo. I'm trying to concentrate," said Tracer, poring over *Trigger*'s sensors. "Hmm. There are indications that alien vessels have arrived at the air base. I wonder what's been going on?"

Zodiac brightened. "Hey, if they've been making, like, first contact, maybe the humans will be cool and hold a welcoming party for us."

He was partly right. The air base had organized a party, but not the welcoming kind.

WHHHHHOOOOSSHHHH!

BANG!

A surface-to-air missile skimmed across *Trigger*'s port side and exploded.

"Ow!" moaned the ship. "That *hurt*!"

Another missile exploded in front of *Trigger*. The ship shook violently from side to side.

"I hate bangs!" moaned Zodiac. "They're noisy and lead to blood and stuff like that." He buried his head in his hands. "Oh, dude, what a bummer!"

Three F15 fighters appeared from behind *Trigger*, cannons blazing.

"Helppppppp!" screamed *Trigger*. "What have I done to them? Why are they shooting at me? Nobody likes me. I should never have left my systems programmer."

"Ship!" snapped Tracer. "I urgently suggest you take defensive action."

"I can't!" sobbed *Trigger*. "I'm just useless!"

"Just take us straight up, you idiot machine!" howled Tracer. "Whoosh factor six."

"Ooooh!" said *Trigger* wonderingly. "I never thought of that."

The F15 pilots gasped in amazement as the spaceship directly in their sights disappeared in the blink of an eye.

Back on board *Trigger*, Tracer gave a sigh of relief. "Why do I have to do all the thinking on this ship?" He gave Zodiac a hard look. "Oh, yes. Now I remember." He drummed eighteen claws on the scanner console. "I wonder where those humans are hiding."

Stonehenge, Salisbury Plain, England

"So what do we do now?" asked Loaf glumly. "Sit here?"

"Not a good idea," said Googie. "The hunters will soon pick up our trail. They could be here any minute."

"We need to ask Help." Jack set The Server down on one of the fallen stones and waited. The hologram showed no signs of appearing.

"Help?" repeated Jack. "Can you come out?"

A note flashed on the screen:

noT uNtil thE pRimAte saYs He's sOrry.

"Say sorry, Loaf," said Jack.

"Why?" moaned Loaf.

"Do it!" everyone shouted.

Loaf sighed. "All right. All right. Sorry," he mumbled.

i cAn't hEar yoU.

"Sorry."

loUdeR!

"SORRY!" screamed Loaf.

Ching! Help shot out. "If love is never having to say you're sorry," it said, "you can safely assume that we ain't ever gonna tie the knot."

Loaf gave a low snarl.

"So whaddaya want now, primates?"

Jack pointed at the stones. "We couldn't find the symbols. "

"Of course you couldn't," replied Help matter-of-factly. "These stones have been around more than three thousand years. The markings have obviously worn off in that time."

"Why . . . didn't . . . you . . . tell . . . us?" demanded Merle slowly.

"You . . . didn't . . . ask . . . me," answered Help. "You said, 'How *should* the site be activated?' and I told you. What you should have asked was how you could activate the site. That's the trouble with you semi-evolved life-forms. Muddled thinking."

Jack held up his hand. "We don't have time for this. What do we do?"

The hologram suddenly became helpful. "There's probably still some residual markings left on the stones, but you'd only be able to see them in ultrared light."

Jack looked puzzled. "Ultrared? I've heard of ultraviolet and infrared light, but I've never heard of ultrared."

Help's head bobbed from side to side.

"That's because you monkeys haven't discovered it yet. You have to have discovered hyperdrive technology before you discover ultrared."

Googie and Bitz nodded. "He's right."

"Ultrared will pick out the symbols, no problem." The hologram materialized itself a pair of snazzy sunglasses, and stripes of sunblock appeared across its nose and cheeks. "Lighten up, people."

The monument was bathed in a strange purple-red glow. The stones shimmered as their secrets were revealed. Every stone was covered with elaborate symbols — geometric and leaflike shapes with an elaborate pattern of vertical scratches running through them. These were set in complex groupings above, below, and cutting through straight horizontal lines, which stood out against the gray of the rock.

Jack studied the patterns. "Celtic knots," he said. "But I don't know what those scratches are."

"Primitive writing," drawled Help. "I'll have to decode it. Childishly simple, of course,

for an artificial intelligence with my process-
ing capacity."

"Then you'd better get started." Merle's
voice was tense. "We've got company."

With a blast of sound, the horseshoe-
shaped craft Merle had seen earlier ripped
through the sky overhead at several times the
speed of sound. As the companions watched,
the vessel slowed and began to turn back
toward them.

Loaf groaned. "Help! Get the lead out, will
ya?"

"I'm working on it, primate. Don't rush
me." Help hummed to itself.

Merle's phone rang. She gave Jack an incredulous glance as she hauled it out of her
pocket. "If this is some dumb telemarketing
call . . ." She flipped it open. "Hello? *Dad?*
Yeah, I'm fine . . ." She eyed the approaching
hunter's craft and added, ". . . ish. You got the
phones working? That's neat. I'm at Stonehenge." Merle dived for cover as an energy
weapon cut a broad swathe in her direction
through the grass and hit a fallen stone, which
shattered. "Listen, I can't talk right now. We're

being shot at by an alien spaceship. Catch you later."

The ship was turning for another pass. At the same time, three more vessels appeared, coming in from varying points of the compass.

"That's it!" Suddenly, the ultrared light Help was producing focused on two lines of script, lying above and below a single Celtic knot. "I got a translation. This is what it says."

Words appeared on the screen behind Help.

> *Touch here*
> *and stand back.*

Help beamed. "I'm so brilliant, sometimes I even surprise myself."

Without replying, Jack hurled himself at the illuminated symbol and pressed it.

A faint roar sounded deep within the stone, then gave out. Jack pressed again, harder this time. There was a series of *chugs* that sounded like an old, run-down car starting up after a long night in the rain. The stones began to hum. The sound built rapidly in pitch. The air around Jack and the others crackled and buzzed. As the four alien ships converged on the ancient ruin, lines of discharged force shot between the stones, building to a whirlpool of blue-white light.

Tingkat Bumbag, distracted by the light show below, flew her ship straight into one of the other converging vessels. Spinning crazily out of control, her crippled machine plowed into the ground. Simultaneously, the other two bounty hunters' ships smashed into each other head-on and vaporized instantly.

Crawling from her wrecked ship (Tingkat's species was notoriously tough), the bounty hunter watched stone-faced as the whirlpool of energy that spun inside the stones enveloped the companions. In the blink of an eye, her prey had disappeared.

CHAPTER FIVE

The Pyramids, near Cairo, Egypt

Jack, Merle, and Loaf found themselves sitting on some kind of stone bench. Although the sky was completely dark, the air was very warm. Googie was perched on Merle's lap, and Jack felt Bitz's hairy body pressed against his shins. All around them, people were staring at them and chattering excitedly in several different languages, probably discussing their unconventional arrival. Jack hurriedly slammed The Server's lid shut on Help.

"Hey!" protested the hologram in muffled tones. "Who turned out the lights?!"

It was an apt comment. The floodlights over their seats dimmed, and the voices of the crowd died away. Jack whispered to Merle, "Where are we?"

TAN — TON — TAAAAAAAA!

A deafening blast of music slammed the companions back into their seats.

"EGYPT," intoned a booming, amplified voice, "LAND OF THE PHARAOHS, WHERE THE BARREN DESERT IS WASHED BY THE FERTILE WATERS OF THE RIVER NILE."

Spotlights pierced the darkness. Slightly to their right loomed an enormous stone head, a human face with its nose and part of its upper lip missing, framed by a formal headdress. More lights revealed that the head rested on the gigantic body of a lion.

"HERE, THE MAJESTIC SPHINX STANDS ETERNAL GUARD OVER THE CITY OF THE DEAD."

Right in front of them, another sequence of lights revealed a triangular-shaped mountain of rock. Loaf clicked his fingers excitedly. "I know where we are! We're at the pyramids."

Merle gave him a scornful look. "Did you work that out all by yourself?"

"THIS IS THE GREAT PYRAMID OF THE PHARAOH KHUFU," the voice declaimed, "KNOWN TO THE GREEKS AS CHEOPS."

The lights on the pyramid dimmed. Laser beams speared out to form an image of the

Pharaoh Khufu on the side of the Great Pyramid.

Bitz clambered onto Jack's lap and gazed at the light show. "What's happening?"

"Shhhh!" Jack cast nervous glances at the surrounding seats, where people were starting to point at Bitz and nudge one another. "You're a dog, remember?"

"HERE, THE PHARAOH BEGINS HIS JOURNEY TO THE AFTERLIFE, WHILE HIS MORTAL REMAINS ARE GUARDED BY ANUBIS, THE JACKAL-HEADED GOD, AND BASTET, DAUGHTER OF THE SUN GOD RE."

The lasers projected the image of a cat-headed goddess. Googie purred approval. "Say what you like about the ancient Egyptians, they sure knew how to treat cats."

"Okay," whispered Merle, "so we're at the pyramids. Does anybody know what we have to do here?"

"This is the second ancient site," said Googie in a stage whisper. "We have to activate its defensive function and teleport on to the third."

Merle stared at the cat. "And where do we have to be to do that?"

Googie indicated the Great Pyramid with a languid paw. "My guess — in there."

Loaf's jaw dropped. "Mummy!"

Merle stared at him. "You want your mom? How old are you?"

"I mean, there could be a mummy in there!" Loaf's eyes were wide and frightened. "A horrible Egyptian mummy, all bandages and bad news, and if we go disturbing it, it'll curse us, and we'll get eaten by beetles, and . . ."

"Shhhh!" A woman sitting behind Loaf flapped at him with her program.

Jack gripped Loaf's arm tightly. "Shut up. We can't do anything now. There are too many people around." He indicated a number of white-uniformed guards patrolling the fringes of the crowd. "We'll have to sneak out later. Just sit back and enjoy the show."

"MANY TALES ARE TOLD," boomed the recorded voice cheerfully, "OF THE DREAD-FUL FATE OF THOSE WHO TRIED TO STEAL FROM THE PHARAOH'S TOMB."

"Enjoy the show," said Loaf faintly. "Yeah, right."

Stonehenge, Salisbury Plain, England

The bounty hunter from the planet Anubia that had collided with Tingkat had fared better than she had. Its ship was almost intact. It had landed and quickly surveyed the Stonehenge site. As it expected, The Server was not there. And the Anubian was about to climb into its craft when it stiffened. The muzzle of a laser pistol was tickling the hair behind its ear.

The owner of the pistol said, "I need your ship."

Having no sweat glands, the dog-headed Anubian lolled its tongue out and panted nervously. "Tingkat! How're you doing?"

"Not too good," said Tingkat regretfully. "You totaled my ship. That's why I'm taking yours."

The Anubian nodded — very carefully. "Fine, but you'll need me as well."

"I think not."

"I think so. You want to know where our prey has gone?"

The pressure on the Anubian's neck eased very slightly. "Surely," Tingkat said softly, "you weren't thinking of keeping information

about the humans' whereabouts to yourself?"
She clicked her tongue. "Shame on you."

"My species knows of another ancient
site." The Anubian licked its lips nervously.

"Keep talking."

"We built it ourselves, on one of the other
continents of this world. The people who lived
there worshiped my species as gods."

"That shows a certain lack of discrimina-
tion," sneered Tingkat.

"My guess is that the humans and their al-
lies have gone there. I can . . ." The creature
gasped as the pistol was jammed into its neck.
"I mean, *we* can be there in a few minutes."

Tingkat nodded. "Makes sense. Here's the
deal. You fly me to this place, and I'll take The
Server."

"And what's in it for me?" demanded the
Anubian.

"Your life."

The Anubian swallowed hard. "That seems
fair."

Moments after the Anubian ship had blasted
off, *Trigger* arrived. The battered ship wob-
bled as Zodiac's inexpert piloting took it on a

sweep of the stone circle. It hovered for a while over Tingkat's crashed vessel.

Tracer peered down at the wreck and ground his needle-sharp teeth. "It seems we're too late. I suppose we'd better land and see if we can pick up any clues as to where the humans have gone."

"No need, dude." Zodiac pointed at a complex pattern of loops and circles that had been crushed and burned into the grass of an adjoining field. "Crop circle. Check it out. Looks to me like the landing marks of an Anubian ship."

Tracer mused. "If you're right — that's got to happen to you sometimes, I suppose —"

"Hey!"

Tracer nodded. "Then there is only one place they could have gone."

Seconds later, Zodiac's battered ship lurched into motion and climbed falteringly into the night sky.

The Pyramids, near Cairo, Egypt

"AND SO THE PHARAOHS SLEEP UNDER THE WATCHFUL EYES OF THE SPHINX WHILE THE CENTURIES ROLL BY, THEIR PASSING MARKED

ONLY BY THE RESTLESS HEARTBEAT OF THE MAJESTIC NILE."

With blaring brass fanfares and a soaring, wordless chorus, the music ended and the lights dimmed.

Merle's eyes sparkled. "Hey, that was really interesting."

Loaf wriggled in his seat. "I prefer more action. And popcorn."

"You want action?" said Jack in a strained voice. "I think you're about to get it." He pointed.

A moving speck of brilliance appeared over the shoulder of the Great Pyramid, approaching very fast from the northwest. At first it was silent. Then a high-pitched whine made itself heard.

A second later, something big and silver swooped past the Great Pyramid and rocketed over the heads of the audience. The thunderous howl of its passage pounded the eardrums of the crowd. Sand and wastepaper were kicked up, making the air gritty. People shrieked and pointed. Many remained seated, not sure whether this was supposed to be part of the show.

Jack was under no such illusions. "Bounty hunters. They've found us."

The Anubian studied its sensors as its ship turned to make another pass. "I can't locate them. There are too many people."

Tingkat nodded. "Then lose the people. Didn't you say something about a guardian?"

The Anubian drew back its doglike lips in what might have been a smile — or a snarl. "My people left an android life-form to guard the tombs. That was a long time ago, of course."

Tingkat's eyes shone with unholy glee. "Let's see if it still works, shall we?"

The Anubian tapped a series of command codes into its ship's communications console . . .

. . . and down below, in the ancient site at the edge of the desert, the strange composite creature known as the Sphinx stretched — and stood.

Its outer stone cracked, crumbled, and fell away. The ancient cyberbeast shrugged off the remains of its body-shaped coffin and stared around with gleaming, predatory eyes.

Below it and to one side, hundreds of humanoids were running about in all directions, making shrill, squealing noises. The Sphinx lashed its tail and hissed at them. The squeals got louder.

But five figures — three humanoids and two smaller quadrupeds — had detached themselves from the rest and were running full speed across the desert, making for the largest of the pyramids that the Sphinx had guarded for so long.

The creature gave a yowl of rage that shook windows five miles away and plunged in pursuit.

Merle's phone rang as she ran. She grabbed it from her jacket pocket and pressed the TALK key.

"Hi, Dad. Look, this isn't a great time right now. . . ." Merle ran with both hands clasped to her head, one holding her phone, the other pressed against her ear so she could hear her father's distant voice against the infuriated roars of the pursuing creature. "Yeah, we got away, but they caught up with us again. We're being chased by the Sphinx. The Sphinx.

S-p-h-i-n-x. You know, two hundred feet long, weighs about a million pounds, woman's head, lion's body. Yeah! Hang on, I'm gonna lose you, we're going into a pyramid. *Py-ra-mid.* Oh, nuts!"

She flipped the phone closed and dodged to the side as the Sphinx pounced. In spite of its catlike agility, the android guardian was too massive to turn quickly. By the time it had changed direction, Merle was panting up the steps to the small entrance to the Great Pyramid. She joined the others in a narrow passage. The Sphinx's yowls of frustration from outside dislodged fragments of stone from the ceiling. Merle held out the phone. "I knew bringing this thing was a bad idea. Now what?"

Jack shook a barred steel door. "It's locked. We can't get in."

"Am-a-teurs." Though Loaf was winded by the long run through soft sand, he wasn't too exhausted to pass up an opportunity to be the center of attention. "Step . . . aside." He took a piece of bent wire from his bag and set to work on the lock. Seconds later, he was rewarded with a sharp click, and the door swung open. Loaf stepped aside. *"Ta-daaa!"*

From outside came a ringing command. The Sphinx hissed. Jack peered out and grabbed Loaf's arm with renewed urgency. "Come on!"

"What's your hurry?" protested Loaf. "That thing is mean, but it's way too big to get in here."

"It's got backup," Jack reported. "The woman who nearly caught us in Ops and some guy with a dog's head, and they *aren't*."

"Aren't what?"

"Too big to get in here. Come *on*!"

The first corridor led downward. After stumbling in the dark for a couple of seconds, Jack flipped open The Server. "Help!"

The hologram appeared. "Hey, primate! Where are we now? It's as dark as a tomb in here!"

"Well spotted," said Jack tightly. "How about some light?"

"For you, anything," sneered Help. But it closed its eyes and blew out its hologrammatic cheeks as if concentrating, and its head began to glow with the radiance of a dim light-bulb.

The companions found themselves standing at the junction of two corridors. One continued to descend, the other climbed away into darkness.

"Down," asked Jack, "or up?"

"Up," grunted Loaf, repressing a shudder.

Jack shrugged and started to climb. At first the passageway was narrow and very low, but after they passed another junction the passage opened up and the roof soared to more than four times human height. Spurred on by noises from the passage below, the companions clambered up the forty-five-degree slope with all the speed they could muster.

At length they stopped, gasping, in a chamber large enough to hold a double-decker bus. A huge, lidless sarcophagus lay to one side of the chamber. Loaf drew back from it. Merle hoisted herself up and peered inside.

"Relax," she told Loaf cheerfully. "Nobody home."

Jack stared around at the featureless walls. "There's nothing here!"

"Hey, Help!" snapped Bitz. "You want to bring on the ultrared again?"

"Work, work, work!" grumbled Help, but it materialized a set of sunglasses and bathed the room with the red-purple color the companions had first seen at Stonehenge. Almost immediately, glowing patterns began to emerge on the walls of the chamber: bewildering rows of objects, people, and animals.

"Hieroglyphics," said Merle. "I did a school project on these." She picked up Googie, who for once made no protest. The cat wanted to see the picture writing close up.

"C'mon, Help!" snapped Bitz. "Which one do we press?"

"Give me time, will ya?" demanded Help. "Now, lemme see. Accessing Rosetta stone files. If the mouth shape is the sound *r* and the owl means *he*, then . . . got it," snapped Help. "Press that symbol." The ultrared light focused on a beautifully detailed carving of a human eye.

Merle gasped. "The Eye of Horus," she whispered. "The symbol of protection against evil. I should have guessed."

"But you didn't. And now, time's up!" The new voice came from the entrance to the chamber.

Jack turned slowly. Behind him, the bounty hunter who called herself Tingkat Bumbag stood alongside a human figure with the head of a dog — or a jackal.

Tingkat leveled an energy weapon at the companions. "Give me The Server."

Seeing Tingkat's companion, Merle wondered whether she'd been wise to make light of ancient superstition. "Anubis," she said. "The jackal-headed god, guardian of the dead."

But the alien's mouth was also open, and it was staring in utmost horror at the small creature in Merle's arms.

"Bastet," it whined. "My ancient enemy, the terror of my people."

Remembering the commentary at the light show, Merle caught on. She held Googie up. "It thinks you're a rival god," she whispered in the cat's ear. "It's totally spooked. Go get it."

With a *meow* of acknowledgment, Googie leaped lightly from Merle's arms and stalked toward the quaking Anubian. The jackal-headed creature gave a strangled howl of fear and turned to run; colliding as it did so with Tingkat. The two bounty hunters went down in a heap.

"Go, Googie!" Merle whooped. "Ol' Bastet must have been hot stuff!"

Jack dived for the eye symbol and pressed it just as Tingkat thrust aside the gibbering Anubian and grabbed her weapon. Too late. Jack, his companions, and The Server were bathed in blue-white light. Their bodies dissolved into a dense cloud of particles that flew around the chamber, bouncing off all four walls before disappearing with a faint whooshing noise up a shaft set high in one of the walls.

Tingkat lowered her weapon and gave the shaking Anubian a furious glare. "Fool!" she spat. "You have robbed me of my opportunity." Her mouth twisted. "I wonder what would have happened if they'd pressed the wrong symbol?"

Tingkat's arm lashed out to press a snake carving. For a moment, nothing happened. Then, with a grinding roar, the solid floor in front of the fading inscriptions split in half, parted slightly, and swung downward. A leopardlike leap carried Tingkat to safety. Her companion, less agile, disappeared into the blackness below with an inhuman shriek.

Tingkat stared into the void for a moment. She whispered, "Fascinating."

She turned on her heel and left the chamber.

The Anubian lay on its back, aching in every limb, and groaned. After a while, it dragged itself onto one elbow, fumbled a small plasma torch from its belt, switched it on, and looked around.

It gave a low whine of terror. It was in a tiny chamber, surrounded by cats. Cat statues lined the walls, gazing aloofly down at their ancient foe. The bundles occupying the spaces between the statues could only be mummified cats. The Anubian whimpered.

Shortly afterward, the breath choked in its throat. There were rustlings in the darkness. Some of the bandaged forms seemed to have developed eyes.

The cat mummies were coming to life.

CHAPTER SIX

Chichén Itzá, Mexico

Jack, Merle, Loaf, Bitz, and Googie emerged in a room with stone walls. Dim light seeped through the doorway behind them.

Loaf sighed. "Why can't we ever land in a hamburger joint?"

There was a loud hiss, and something long, wriggly, and scaly scuttled between Loaf's legs. He leaped into the air and gave a falsetto scream. Then he threw himself back against the wall and clutched at his heart. "What — what — what?"

"Looked like an iguana," said Merle off-handedly. "That would put us somewhere in the Americas."

"Well, thank you, Doctor Doolittle," snarled Loaf. "While you're playing I spy with the local wildlife, I'm having a major coronary episode here. I thought we'd stumbled onto another low-life alien."

Merle shook her head. "Nope. That was one of our genuine homegrown monsters. I wonder where we are now."

Bitz trotted toward the barely visible door-way through which the lizard had escaped. "Let's go find out."

They stepped out from a round building with a cone-shaped stone roof, set on a square base. Jack blinked in the sudden light. The sun was high in a sky dotted with fleecy white clouds. It was warm and more humid than their last stopover in Egypt.

The companions looked around. They were in a ruined city. Timeworn buildings in gray stone rose from grass-covered fields sur-rounded by trees. Everywhere, brightly dressed tourists strolled about, took photographs, or followed in the wake of bustling guides who wore hats and carried small flags.

"Popular spot," drawled Loaf. "How about we find an English-speaking guide and tag along? Find out what this place is?"

"No need." Merle's voice was strange. Jack looked at her quickly. "I know where we are,"

Merle continued. "Dad brought us here when we were stationed at Edwards — me and Mom — just before she . . . died." The hesitation was slight. Merle gave Jack a quick it's-okay smile. She gestured at the majestic ruins. "We're in Mexico. This is Chichén Itzá." She scowled at Loaf. "Before you ask, that isn't some kind of fast food. This is one of the great cities of the Maya."

Loaf spread his hands. "I wasn't going to say nothin'!"

Merle gestured to the building behind them. "We arrived in the Caracol. It's supposed to be some kind of Stone Age observatory, I think." She pointed to a tiered building flanked by a forest of ramrod-straight columns that marched like a stone army into the jungle behind it. "That's the Temple of the Warriors, and over there is the ball court."

Loaf whistled. "These guys played football? Wild!"

"Not American football, you bonehead." Merle gave Loaf a disgusted look. "A ball game wasn't just a sporting event for the Maya. It was a ritual. It was where men played hardball with the gods. It was *sacred*."

Loaf puffed out his chest, showing off his New York Giants shirt. "Well, excuuuse me! Are you implying that NFL *isn't*?"

Merle rolled her eyes and pointed to the highest building in the complex. It rose majestically above the other ruins. Its four-stepped, triangular sides were bisected by towering stone stairways. A squat temple with a dark, pillared doorway in each of its four walls sat brooding on its flattened top.

"And that," said Merle, "is El Castillo. My guess is, it's where we'll find the third ancient site."

Loaf gave a hollow groan. "Oh, no! Not *more* pyramids."

The Pyramids, near Cairo, Egypt

Tracer, wearing a robe that concealed his non-human shape from casual observers, regarded the collapsed Sphinx and tried to ignore the peddler who kept trying to sell him things. The gigantic android had expired with the departure of the Anubian ship. Now it lay motionless, surrounded by curious Egyptians, stunned guards, and tourists who were clearly trying to cope with far more culture shock that they'd bargained for.

The peddler waved a strip of brightly colored pictures in front of Tracer's face. "My friend! Do you want to buy a postcard?" Tracer shook his head, grimly regretting the almost universal command of languages that went with his former job and allowed him to understand the man's sledgehammer sales pitch. "Mineral water? It's very good, and very cold." Tracer irritably waved him away.

Zodiac ambled over. "Hey, man, ask him if he saw the kids."

Tracer sighed but put the question to the peddler, who nodded eagerly. "Oh, yes, my friend. Just now, I saw the god Anubis go into the pyramid, following three young tourists and a dog and a cat — and" — he paused significantly — "and a strange-looking woman with green hair and green skin."

Tracer hissed through his teeth. "Tingkat Bumbag! The most ruthless bounty hunter of them all."

Zodiac raised his eyebrows. "Yeah? Sounds like a real hot babe."

Tracer turned back to the peddler. "Did they all come back out again?"

The man shook his head. "Oh, no. Only the strange woman came out."

"Then we are too late." Tracer stormed off toward the dark corner where they had parked *Trigger*. Zodiac had to run to keep up. "Tingkat must have double-crossed the Anubian and stolen his ship," Tracer announced after some thought. "The pyramid is armed — your instruments picked that up when we were still a thousand miles away — so Jack Armstrong and his friends have been here, and if they did not leave the pyramid, they must have teleported to their next destination."

As they approached Zodiac's ship, a nightmarish howl of fear and agony rose from the depths of the Great Pyramid and echoed across the desert. Zodiac shivered. "Hey, man, like, what was that?"

"The Anubian finding his way into the afterlife," said Tracer without breaking stride, "if I'm any judge."

"Whoa. Sounds like a real drag." Zodiac followed Tracer through *Trigger*'s main hatchway, nodding intelligently. "So, like, what *is* the next destination?"

Tracer logged on to the Outernet. His nimble claws flew over the touch-sensitive keys of *Trigger*'s main computer console. "Thematic link. Pyramids. They will have gone to another pyramid, on another continent." Images appeared on the screen. Tracer nodded grimly. "There are several possibilities. We have some searching to do."

Zodiac nodded. "Okay, dude, you got it. Do we have time to stop for pizza?" Tracer shook his head. "Drive through?"

"No."

Zodiac slumped in the pilot's seat. "You are one mean dude."

Trigger rose erratically into the sky and headed west.

Chichén Itzá, Mexico

The companions had climbed the steep steps to the top of El Castillo. Loaf had complained every step of the way. Then, when they'd entered the temple at the pyramid's top, they'd had to wait a long time until it was clear of tourists.

Now, finally, they were alone. Jack opened The Server. "Help."

The hologram popped into view. "Oh, mercy!" said Help sarcastically. "Another cheery location. Have you monkeys ever thought of spending some time on the beach? Or maybe going into the home improvement business?"

"Less lip," Merle told it firmly, "and more ultrared."

Help scowled. "I was just trying to lighten the atmosphere. No need to be so touchy." But its sunglasses reappeared. The chamber was flooded with the strange light, and once again patterns began to form.

"Mayan glyphs," said Merle authorita-tively. Loaf stared at her. Merle shrugged. "I don't know much about them except they're a kind of picture writing, like Egyptian hiero-glyphics. Each of those little square pictures is a word. It's a pretty tough language — it took the experts years to decipher."

Loaf nodded wisely. "So we need Help to

figure out the instructions to activate the site and t-mail us to the next one."

Help groaned. "Oh, my aching processors! Okay, okay." The grouchy hologram materialized itself a Sherlock Holmes getup, complete with a deerstalker hat, a droopy pipe, and an oversized magnifying glass with which it examined the Mayan symbols. "Got it! Elementary, my dear primates." Once more, the light beam focused on a single pattern of symbols. "Press that symbol there." Confidently, Loaf pressed it.

Nothing happened.

A worried look crossed Help's face. "Or maybe it should have been *that* one over *there*."

Without warning, the floor beneath them gave way. Yelling (and barking and meowing) with fright, the companions fell.

They tumbled into darkness, sliding down what seemed to be an enormously long chute. Wisps of stringy material brushed their faces as they fell (Jack thought about giant spider-webs and hoped these were vines).

After a descent that lasted several heart-stopping seconds, they tumbled into soft sand. More shocked than hurt, they picked themselves up.

"Is everyone okay?" asked Merle.

Googie hissed. "That was *so* undignified — and I think I broke a claw."

"Is that all?" Loaf rubbed his backside and winced. "Lucky you." He turned to their holo-grammatic helpmate. "Wait until I get my hands on you," he growled.

"Whoops!" Help turned pale. "The man-agement cannot be held responsible for any-thing at all. The value of your investments may go down as well as up. Absolutely no guarantees, exchanges, refunds, or credits will be given." It blew Loaf a kiss and van-ished.

Jack picked up The Server and looked around. "Wow," he said.

They stood in a cavern of enormous pro-portions. Huge stalactites hung glistening from the roof that soared above them, like the inside of a mighty cathedral. Sunlight poured through a single hole amid the petrified stone icicles and shone on a deep blue underground lake.

Merle moved to Jack's side. "They call these places *cenotés*. Some of them are open to tourists, but I never saw one this big. I guess maybe nobody's discovered it yet."

"Nobody human, to be precise," said a strange, hissing voice from somewhere behind them.

"Loaf," said Merle without turning around, "who just said that?"

"I don't know," said Loaf in a far-off voice. "What would you call a gigantic snake with feathers and wings?"

Merle remained rooted to the spot. "I'm not sure," she said faintly. "A winged serpent, I guess."

"Oh. Well, there's a winged serpent behind you."

Merle and Jack turned around and gazed openmouthed at the strange creature that reared up halfway to the cavern roof, maintaining its balance with unhurried beats of its great wings. "Quetzalcoatl," whispered Merle.

The creature blinked in the disconcerting way of snakes. "Quet-zal-co-atl," it said slowly. "Yes, that was one of my many names. I was also known as Ku-kul-can by the people of the city above — many years ago." It gave a rather sad little sigh.

Merle found herself at a loss. "Are you a god?" she asked.

The creature put its snake head on one side. "No. At least, I don't think so. Though I've often been mistaken for one. I've been here an awfully long time, you see."

"How long?" demanded Bitz bluntly.

"Well, let me think." Quetzalcoatl mused. "Around four thousand Earth years or so." It ignored the companions' gasps and exclamations. "Yes, that's about right, I think. It's fortunate that I am of a long-lived species. It's been such a long task, you see."

Jack caught on. "So — you're an alien."

"Oh, I'm not native to Earth." The gigantic creature giggled. "Obviously."

"You mentioned a task," said Bitz. "What task?"

"My project." The winged snake drew itself up proudly, until its head nearly disappeared among the stalactites high above. "I am a scientist. My species gave me a grant to pursue a project to understand the human race."

Googie gave Quetzalcoatl an inscrutable

cat stare. "And this project of yours has been going on for four thousand *years*?"

The strange being deflated. Suddenly, it looked sheepish. "Well," it said in subdued tones, "I didn't *plan* it that way. I was supposed to deliver my report millennia ago. But whenever I thought I'd finished it, humans kept coming up with behavior I just couldn't believe. So I'd have to study that, of course. And then, later, they started bringing me specimens."

Merle stared at Quetzalcoatl with narrowed eyes. "Specimens? As in human specimens?"

"Of course." Quetzalcoatl seemed surprised at the question.

Merle wondered exactly how the snake creature had gotten its "specimens" and decided she really didn't want to know. "Come on," she ordered her friends. "We're leaving."

With amazing speed for a creature of its size, Quetzalcoatl blocked their way. "Oh, I think not," it hissed. There was nothing friendly or vague about the black snake eyes now. "You see, my people stopped bringing me specimens several hundred years ago, and I've finished cataloging all those I have. I require more material for my studies — and since you have been kind enough to present yourselves to me . . ." The creature broke off, having noticed that Loaf was edging toward the cave exit. "I really wouldn't try to escape if I were you. I assure you, I am extremely venomous." It bared fangs that were longer and sharper than most swords. "I suggest cooperation."

There was a crash of thunder. The earth shook. A couple of stalactites fell from the roof of the cave and buried their points in the floor. The companions staggered, and Quetzalcoatl fell flat on its nose. A cloud of dust billowed through the passageway into the first cave.

"My cave," hissed the infuriated serpent. "Someone has discovered my cave!" It folded its wings and shot through the narrow passageway at amazing speed.

Jack looked around. "Quick — while it's gone! That thing must have had a way of bringing its *specimens* down here."

It was Bitz who found the freight elevator, a plain door of some alien substance molded to look like stone. The controls were simple. Once they'd piled into the narrow space and the door had shut behind them, one push of a button with an arrow pointing up sent them into an uncomfortably fast ascent.

The companions emerged in the center of the temple they had so abruptly left only a few minutes ago, giving a group of Italian tourists the shock of their lives. Racing out into the open air, they stood on top of the pyramid and stared out in amazement over the ruins.

Far below, tourists were rushing for shelter, except for a few foolhardy ones who were trying to take pictures. In the skies above, a strange battle was being fought. Tingkat had arrived. Her sensors had located The Server in an underground cavern, but in trying to blast a way through to its location she had disturbed a large and savage creature that seemed to have taken grave exception to her presence.

Tingkat, in her stolen ship, was trying everything she knew to get Quetzalcoatl in her sights; but the infuriated snake creature slid through the air as an eel does through water and was proving twice as slippery. Bursts of fire and screeches of rage rolled over the ancient stones of the Mayan city.

Merle's phone rang. She flipped it open.

"Hi, Dad. Yes, I'm fine. I was about to become a lab specimen for an alien masquerading as a snake god, but it got called away on business. Where am I? On top of a pyramid. No, not that pyramid, another pyramid. Yes, I did say snake god. It's kinda preoccupied right now; it's having a fight with a spaceship. Whoa! That thing is fast! Listen, I'll catch up with you later, okay? We have things to do. Bye."

Jack led the way back into the temple and called for Help. "Now," he told the hologram, "let's try that again. And no foul-ups this time, okay?"

Help scowled. "Gee, one little mistake." It saw the looks on its friends' faces. "Okay, okay. It's a tough language, I think one of you mentioned that. Press that picture over there."

Jack's hand hovered over the glyph. "This one?"

"Yup."

"Sure?"

"Sure, I'm sure."

"You were sure last time."

"Sue me. This time I'm double certain sure."

Hesitantly, Jack pressed his hand on the

picture. Immediately, the hum they had first heard at Stonehenge sounded from beneath them. A moment later, the site was activated, and with a flare of blue-white light, the companions were gone.

Tingkat was finding her opponent too hot to handle. The winged serpent was faster and much more maneuverable than the clumsy Anubian ship. A glancing blow sent the bounty hunter twisting through the air, yawing violently. As Tingkat fought desperately for control, Quetzalcoatl, the snake god, plunged roaring in pursuit, closing in for the kill.

CHAPTER SEVEN

Uluru, Northern Territory, Australia

"That is one heck of a lump of rock!" exclaimed Loaf, craning his neck in a futile attempt to take in the huge sandstone mass that stood against the dawn sky. "But at least it isn't another pyramid."

Merle checked her phone. "There's no reception — wherever we are, it's in the middle of nowhere."

"It's Ayers Rock," said Jack. "I've seen pictures. We're in the middle of Australia."

The companions took in their latest surroundings. The rock thrust up out of a pancake-flat desert scrubland of sand, grass, and bushes. A heavy smell of eucalyptus hung on the early morning air.

The sun rose, causing the rock to change

color. The monolith slowly transformed from a dull gray into a dark red hue, as if the sun's warming rays were causing blood to pulse through the very rock itself, bringing it to life.

"So why are we here?" asked Merle. "We're supposed to activate the fourth ancient site, right? So where is it?"

"I don't know," said Jack. "But we aren't alone."

He pointed to an area not too far away, where groups of tourists were gathered around, taking photographs of the sunrise over one of the natural wonders of the world.

Merle gestured at The Server in Jack's hands. "Let's find some place away from the crowds and see if our friendly neighborhood hologram can tell us where this site is."

The group set off on a track that ran around the base of the rock, which stretched for several miles. Its sandstone walls were scarred with ravines, gullies, and small caves. For several minutes they walked in silence. A couple of small red lizards appeared, scooting from holes and crevices to bathe in the rays of the rising sun.

Suddenly, Bitz pricked his ears and stopped short. "Shhh! Listen." He flattened himself on the ground. Following his example, the others crouched low. There was a low, resonant drone coming from one of the small gullies in the rock. It had an unearthly sound.

"A spaceship?" asked Merle.

"Could be a bounty hunter," said Googie, lashing her tail.

"But how could they be here already?" Jack whispered.

The droning grew louder. Mixed with the underlying hum, the companions could make out the cry of animals and the call of birds. Barks, yowls, yelps, squawks, chirps, and croaks filled the air. The sound became more urgent.

Jack snapped his fingers. "I know what it is!" he exclaimed. Hurrying toward the noise, he beckoned to the others. "Come on." Cautiously, they followed him into the sandstone gully, toward the source of the noise.

At the end of the gully, sitting cross-legged on a ledge, was a white-haired, bearded Aborigine. The old man was blowing into a long, hollowed-out tree trunk that rested on his bare legs.

"A didgeridoo!" announced Jack. "That's what the sound was."

"It'll never replace music," muttered Loaf.

The Aborigine seemed unaware of the companions. He continued to play his ancient instrument. A cacophony of sounds resonated through the morning air.

As he listened to the almost primeval sounds, Jack studied the wiry figure before him. He was bare chested and wore only a few scraps of leather around his waist. Deep lines of experience and knowledge were etched into his dark face. Bushy white eyebrows hid his eyes. Loaf turned to Jack and whispered, "There's something strange about this guy — he's not breathing!"

The man suddenly stopped playing and looked up with a grin. "No, mate. I blow and take in air through my nose at the same time. Circular breathing, see." He blew a few notes to demonstrate.

Loaf raised an eyebrow. "That's some trick! Imagine being able to eat a king-size double cheeseburger without having to breathe between bites." A dreamy, faraway look crossed his face.

The old man set aside the wooden instrument. "G'day. The name's Albert. I been expecting you."

Jack looked puzzled. "How did you know we were coming?"

In reply, the old man smiled. "Uluru is a place where many paths and trails cross."

Loaf glared at Jack. "I thought you said this place was called Ayers Rock."

"That's what the settlers called it," said the old man peaceably. "We Aborigines call it Uluru. I reckon your *iwara* brought you here."

"Our what?" asked Merle.

"Your *iwara* — your path. Just like my *iwara* — my ancestors' path — brought me."

"Oh! You've been teleporting around the planet, too?" asked Loaf sarcastically. Merle gave him a sharp dig with her elbow.

Albert chuckled. "There's more than one way to fly around the planet, mate," he said enigmatically. "Fancy something out my dilly bag?" He reached into a bark carryall by his side, pulled out a cloth, and unfolded it. It was full of grubs and beetles. "Bush tucker," he explained. "Anyone for breakfast?"

Merle, Jack, and Googie all politely declined. Loaf stared at the food in horror. "I'll just take the fries."

Bitz licked his chops. "What's to eat?"

Albert picked up a couple of large white wriggly things and held them before Bitz's nose. "Witchety grubs."

Bitz gulped — and grinned. "Tasty. Keep 'em coming!"

The others watched, squirming, as Bitz and Albert ate breakfast. "Do you know why your path has led you here?" asked Albert between wriggly mouthfuls.

"We're using the ancient sites to travel," replied Jack. "We have to find the next one."

The Aborigine gestured around him "You've found it, mate. The site is Uluru itself."

Loaf curled his lip. "How can a rock be an ancient site? It's not as if someone built it."

Albert gave Loaf a pitying stare. It was a look born of the knowledge of thousands of years, passed down from generation to generation. "Sure they did, mate. Uluru was formed in the Dreamtime, the time of creation, when our ancestors sang into existence the people, the land, and everything."

Loaf raised a disbelieving eyebrow but said nothing.

"Who are you?" asked Merle.

The man smiled. "Like I said, the name's Albert. I'm one of the Anangu — the people." He patted the rock. "You wanted to find the ancient site. This is it. And I'm one of its caretakers." He nodded at Jack. "Just like you are," he said, pointing at The Server.

Jack wondered how Albert knew about his task. "You're not The Weaver, are you?" he asked.

Albert gave a chuckle. "Here, everything is woven together — the land, the law, the people, the creatures." He shook his head. "No, mate. I'm not The Weaver."

"But can you help us?" Merle asked.

Albert considered. When at last he spoke, his voice was solemn. "On Uluru, there are sacred sites where only a chosen few may enter." He stood up. "I reckon you've been chosen. Follow me."

Chichén Itzá, Mexico

Zodiac watched the battle between Tingkat and Quetzalcoatl rage above the jungle. "Looks like the green babe is in trouble."

"Good," said Tracer offhandedly. "Her attacker is an Aspian. I wonder what it's doing on Earth." He gave a multiarmed shrug. "Well, it's no concern of ours. The creature isn't bothering us. Take us in while it's finishing her off."

"Man, were you always this mean, or did you take advanced classes?" Zodiac angled *Trigger* toward the pyramid far below, immediately attracting Quetzalcoatl's attention.

"Oh, no!" squealed *Trigger*. "It's attacking *me* now!" With a howl of overloaded engines, the overwrought vessel pulled away from the flying serpent's clutches in a tight high-g turn and shot wildly into the sky.

"Turn back and arm your weapons," snarled Tracer. "We'll teach the Aspian some manners."

"Sorry, dude." Zodiac looked sheepish. "No can do. This is a peace-loving, environmentally friendly ship. It don't have no weapons."

Tracer slapped himself on the forehead. Six times. "Of all the millions of spaceships in the Galaxy, I end up on this worn-out, powerless pile of junk!"

"You'll be sorry you said that," wailed *Trigger*.

Tracer turned on Zodiac. "I thought you were supposed to be a space desperado."

Zodiac shrugged. "Dude, I'm desperate most of the time. Mostly, I'm desperate to stay out of trouble!"

The Aspian continued to circle above the pyramid, guarding its lair. Tracer considered the situation for a moment before opening up a communications channel. An image of Tracer's rival appeared on *Trigger*'s viewscreen.

Tracer gave an ironic bow. "Tingkat."

Tingkat's face momentarily betrayed surprise. "Well, well. Tracer. What brings you to this neck of the Galaxy? Don't tell me you're after The Server for yourself?"

Tracer ignored Tingkat's questions. "I have a proposal for you to consider."

"Propose away. I'm listening."

"Sensors indicate that this site has been activated, which means our prey is getting away. The longer we wait here, the cooler the trail will be. Therefore, I suggest that my vessel should distract the Aspian while you take the opportunity to ruffle its feathers. In the most literal sense," he added.

Trigger moaned. "I hate this plan already!" it said. Zodiac burrowed his head in his hands.

Tingkat raised a green eyebrow. "And then?"

"And then we meet at the pyramid and continue the hunt."

Tingkat slowly nodded agreement. "I advise you not to double-cross me, or you'll be next on my list."

Tracer looked hurt. "Tingkat — as if I would."

Despite protests from *Trigger* and Zodiac, Tracer ordered the ship to head for the Aspian. Weeping with terror, *Trigger* skimmed the creature, buzzing and flitting around it like an annoying mosquito. Quetzalcoatl roared and lashed at the ship with its whiplike tail until Tingkat came shooting out and launched a plasma-bolt attack that sent Quetzalcoatl, keening with shock and pain, plunging back through the entrance to its hidden cave. The battle was over.

Fifteen minutes later, Tracer and Zodiac were standing in the empty chamber at the top of El Castillo.

"Where did the green chick go?" asked Zodiac.

"Mr. Hobo, when Tingkat arrives, I suggest that you do not refer to her as *chick* unless you want to lose several useful parts of your body."

Zodiac gave Tracer a conspiratorial nudge. "Feisty gal, huh? Groovy."

Tracer ignored Zodiac. "Time waits for no being. Let's find out where these humans have taken The Server."

"You can do that?"

Tracer gave Zodiac a contemptuous glare. "During my lifetime, I have traced and monitored billions of communications from the farthest reaches of the Galaxy. This task is small in comparison." He faced the wall and placed his six claws on the glyphs.

Zodiac looked puzzled. "Hey, dude, hugging rocks, that's kinda cosmic, but how's that gonna tell us where to go?"

"I'm feeling for the afterglow." Tracer's visor pulsed red. "Good. It's still here." He concentrated hard. "Another continent. A rock in the middle of a desert. A place called . . . Australia!"

"Australia! Excellent!"

Tracer and Zodiac spun around as one. Tingkat stood in the doorway. Zodiac's knees turned to jelly. The bounty hunter gave an apologetic wave of the hand. "I got lost."

"Lost?" demanded Tracer. "How? To climb a pyramid, you start at the bottom and continue on up to the top. There are not many places you can get sidetracked."

Tingkat ignored the remark. "So it's a race to The Server. May the best being win. Last one to the other side of the planet is a Sirian slug-sloth." She turned and sprinted out of the chamber.

Zodiac watched her go with a big stupid grin on his face. His eyes were wide-open and his tongue hung out. "Oh, man! What a babe!"

Tracer dragged the drooling space hippie

out the door and down the pyramid. "She's an ice-cold killing machine, and you're a feckless idiot. It would never work." Tracer increased his pace until they had to run to avoid tripping and falling down the steps head over heels. "Come on!" hissed Tracer with low cunning. "The quicker we get to the ship, the quicker you get to see her again."

But on reaching Zodiac's ship, they found *Trigger* in a state of shock.

"Infamy! Infamy! Everyone's got it in for me!" cried the ship. "I've been violated!"

"Tingkat!" Tracer punched at the control panels. They were dead. "She's sabotaged the ship. That's why she was late."

"She — she touched my terminals!" *Trigger* wept. "She fried my chips!"

"Tingkat did this? Oh, man, tell me it ain't so!" Zodiac wailed. "I never want to see her shining green face again! What're we gonna do, dude?"

"Begin repairs. And don't worry." Tracer's visor pulsed brightly. "There's more than one way to catch a Rabbian sleekit cowrin timrous beastie. The clever hunter waits for the prey to come to him."

Uluru, Northern Territory, Australia

The Friends were standing in a small cave. Albert had lit a fire. The orange flames flickered brightly, lighting up the cave walls and revealing strange carvings and paintings. Multicolored and complex patterns intermingled with the shapes of people, animals, and birds.

"They're beautiful," said Merle.

Albert ran a hand across the layers of paint. "They're a connection between the past and present, the people and the land, and" — he paused for a second — "the earthly and unearthly." He turned to Jack. "Reckon you should choose what you need. If it's meant, it'll come to you."

With the others looking on silently, Jack closed his eyes and tried to connect with the rock. Feelings of belonging flooded into him — to the land, the people, and their way of life — their very existence.

And then he knew.

Opening his eyes, he pointed at a picture of concentric circles. "That's it," he said.

Albert clapped his hands in delight. "The

symbol of the dreaming sites. Reckon you were meant to know."

Jack gave the Aborigine a nod of appreciation. "Thank you for your help."

Ching!

Help appeared. "Okay, okay, okay. I know, I know. You're in trouble again, you can't find your way around, you need me, you can't live without me. What have I gotta do for you primates now?"

"Nothing." Merle shook her head. "We've managed by ourselves."

There was a momentary silence. "Excuse me? I thought for a moment there you said you managed to do something for yourselves," Help said in disbelief. "That doesn't compute with me. Obviously, I am becoming delusional from overwork and associating with no-brain life-forms. I'm gonna have to lie down and take the weight off my processors." The hologram disappeared into The Server.

"Nice mate you got," observed Albert. A cloud of sand blew into the cave from outside. Albert gave a sniff. "Reckon you'd better be moving on."

Jack nodded, placed his hand against the chosen symbol, and pushed. It began to glow. All at once the cave was filled with sounds of animals, birds, and people. The shapes seemed to leap off the wall and spin around and around in a dance of unity. *Like N-space*, thought Jack. Then there was a flash of light as the site was activated, and the companions disappeared.

Albert gave a deep sigh and turned to the cave's entrance to greet the new arrival.

"Where are they?"

"I'm afraid you're too late."

Tingkat gave a growl of annoyance. "Where have they gone?"

Albert held out his hands. "Now, as if I'm going to tell you that." With a shake of his head, the old man vanished into thin air before Tingkat's very angry eyes.

She rushed to the wall. It was covered with incomprehensible patterns. She tried to feel for warmth as Tracer had, but there was nothing. Tingkat stood breathing deeply, considering her next move. "This accursed planet," she whispered. A thought struck her. Tracer had mentioned another continent. That was it! Which continents hadn't they yet visited? With a snarl, she rushed out of the cave.

Mountainside, location unknown

The blinding white of the teleportation vortex gave way to the blinding white of a snow-storm. Wind howled, whipping flakes into stinging flurries. The moment the cold hit him, Jack began to freeze.

He could make out nothing but the dark out-lines of steep mountains. Wind-driven snow snapped at his face and froze. The chill air tore at his lungs, freezing him from the inside out. His thin clothes provided no protection. Des-perately, he struggled to walk through the chest-deep snow.

"Merle! Bitz!" he yelled. "Loaf! Googie!"

It was useless. The roar of the storm was all-encompassing.

The snow was piling up into drifts. As the minutes toiled by with agonizing slowness and his body froze, Jack tried to push on, seek-ing the others, shelter, help, but he could hardly move. The cold was mind numbing.

➤ **the hunt**

Jack felt his senses slipping as the snow piled up around him. Shivering uncontrollably, his teeth chattering with cold, he dropped The Server from his frozen fingers and slumped headfirst into white oblivion.

CHAPTER EIGHT

Hidden Valley, Tibet

Jack awoke to the sound of birdsong.

He sat up and looked around in amazement. He had slipped into unconsciousness on a freezing snowfield. Now he was lying on short, wiry grass beneath a tree covered with pink blossoms. Small birds — finches, Jack thought — flitted and squabbled in the branches above, occasionally dislodging petals that tumbled down lazily to join those that had already settled on him.

Jack sat up. How did he get here? With a guilty start, he remembered the others. Where were they? Had they been on the mountain, too? And if so, had they survived the freezing cold? He scrambled to his feet and gazed around, frantically seeking some sign of his friends. That was when he realized that he was not alone.

The man who sat under a nearby tree, gazing serenely into the distance, was dressed in simple, homespun robes. On his head was a hat made of straw. He wore nothing on his feet. In his lap he held The Server.

Jack walked toward him on legs that still ached with fatigue. He tried to move slowly so as not to alarm the old man, but his mind was screaming frantic questions, tumbling over one another with their urgency to be heard. Who was the stranger? Why did he have The Server, and would he be willing to give it up? Were the others okay? Were they here? Come to think of it, where *was* here, and what was Jack himself doing in this strange place?

As Jack approached, the man looked up and gave him a tranquil smile. He held out The Server. "This was found beside you. I assume it is of value to you."

Well, at least that answered the first two of his questions. "Yes. Thank you." Jack took The Server with a great sense of relief and turned it over, running his hands over the

scuffed casing. It didn't look as if it had suffered major damage, and unless the old man
was speaking English (which seemed unlikely), it was still translating. Jack looked into
his eyes. "Thank you," he said again. The old
man smiled and nodded but said nothing.

Jack said, "Are my friends here?"

"They are nearby. The boy, the girl, the —
others. They have not yet awoken."

Jack eyed the speaker with misgivings.
How could he know Merle and Loaf were still
asleep if he couldn't see them? And why did
he call Bitz and Googie "the others"? But Jack
only asked, "Where are we?"

The stranger said, "In my valley."

Jack looked up. They were indeed in a valley. A stream ran through green meadows that
were dotted with wildflowers and groves of
trees. None of the trees were bare of leaves,
and many were in bloom. Birds flew and but-
terflies danced in the still, warm air. And yet
on every side towered great, snow-covered
mountains. The snowfields and glaciers
seemed to end just beyond the farthest trees.
The sun shone over the valley, though the
peaks surrounding it were shrouded in clouds.

The old man rose unhurriedly to his feet. "Your friends are stirring." Picking up a staff that lay in the grass beside him, he made his way unhurriedly down the grassy slope. Wondering but not questioning, Jack followed.

The stranger was right. Loaf and Merle were stretching and looking around in bewilderment. Bitz was sniffing at the unfamiliar scents. Only Googie still lay peacefully asleep, although, Jack reflected, knowing the cat's habits, she might well have woken up earlier and gone back to sleep by choice.

Seeing Jack, Merle stood up and moved toward him, still staring around her. "I think," she said softly, "this is the most beautiful place I've ever seen."

Jack's guide smiled and bowed to Merle as if she had paid him a compliment.

Bitz sniffed at Googie. "You okay, fleabag?"

Googie cracked an eye open and yawned, stretching and unsheathing her claws. "I was until you came and yelled in my ear, dogbreath." But there was no heat in the insults, and the rival chameleoids sat side by side as they studied their surroundings.

Loaf's first words were, "What's to eat? I'm

hungry!" His voice was unusually subdued, and he looked around him with an air of appreciation that was at odds with his usual bad temper.

The old man gave him a placid smile. "If you will come with me, you will share my food."

"Burgers?" asked Loaf, more in hope than anticipation. "Doughnuts?"

The stranger shook his head. "I am a poor hermit. I have only milk, butter, and cheese, honey, fruits, and bread."

"Oh, great," muttered Loaf. "New Age slop." But his complaint lacked its usual venom, and he trudged after the others willingly enough.

The hermit's home turned out to be a one-room dwelling made from white stone, with a sloping roof of red, sun-dried tiles. A woven grass curtain covered the doorway and reed mats lay on the floor. Inside, a straw pallet served as a bed. There was a low table in the center of the room but no chairs, and a brick oven against one wall where (the old man told them) he baked his bread.

The companions and their guide ate their simple meal in silence broken only by the occasional bleating of a small herd of sheep and goats that grazed placidly nearby. They used their bread to scoop soft cheese and honey from the earthenware jars in which they were stored and drank goat's milk straight from the pitcher.

When even Loaf had declared himself satisfied, they moved outside to sit in the sunshine and gaze out over the valley. After a while, Jack turned to the hermit and said, "Did you bring us here? From the mountain?"

"I?" The old man looked down at his small-framed body and smiled. "No. That was my companion."

"I thought you lived alone here." Merle was surprised.

"I do, and I do not." The old man watched a hawk sweeping circles in the sky above the valley. "My companion is always here, yet he and I have never met."

"That doesn't make sense!" protested Loaf.

"Much is not what it seems," said the hermit peaceably. He looked pointedly at Bitz and

Googie, who (surprisingly) were managing to lie close together without fighting. "Many are not what they appear to be."

Jack wanted to ask how the stranger knew that Googie and Bitz were not really a cat and a dog and was wondering how to do it without admitting to their real identities when Loaf broke in. "What is this place, anyway?" He waved his arm across the valley. "It should be cold, but it's warm. It's snowing on the mountains, but the sun's shining here. What gives?"

For a moment, it seemed as if the old hermit would not respond, but at length, he said, "I am one of the last of my kind. We were never very many — not since the land of my ancestors disappeared beneath the ice."

Loaf nudged Merle. "Does he mean Atlantis?" Merle shushed him angrily. The old man appeared not to notice the interruption. He continued.

"Once, my people helped yours to build their cities and gave them the secrets of tools to till their fields. But they turned their cities into fortresses and their tools into weapons and fought one another until we knew we

could not live among them. And so we retreated here, to the high and lonely places of
the world, and crafted refuges for ourselves
that only we could see."

"Then you must have been here for a long
time," Merle said slowly. "Hundreds — maybe
thousands of years."

The old man shrugged. "What is time?"

Merle stared at him. "Are you telling us
you are not human?"

Once more, their guide ignored the question.

"Will we see your companion?" asked
Merle.

The hermit smiled faintly. "Perhaps. He
only appears by the light of the moon. At other
times, he cannot be seen."

Merle gave the man a distrustful look. "Are
we talking about the supernatural here?
Magic?"

The hermit chuckled softly. "Humans! You
divide the world into that which can be seen
and that which cannot. You measure that
which does not matter and give it importance
because you can measure it. You divide natural from supernatural, science from magic.
Then you worship the one and deny the

other." He chuckled again. "So narrow. So foolish." A faraway look crept into his eyes.

"This is crazy talk," Loaf whispered to Jack. "Strange powers — invisible companions. The old guy's been up here for too long. He's totally nutso!"

"He saved us," Jack hissed back. "Or his friend did. At any rate, he's looked after us and given us food. We owe it to him to show some respect." Loaf retreated, muttering.

Jack turned to their host. "I think we have something to do here," he said hesitantly. "We have to activate five ancient sites to protect Earth. We are looking for the last site, but we are being followed by dangerous enemies who would destroy your valley in an instant and think nothing of it if they thought it would get them what they wanted."

The old man stirred. His face broke into a gentle smile. "As for my valley, do not concern yourself. As for your task — follow me." He stood up in the same unhurried way he did everything and was about to lead them off when Merle put a hand on his arm.

"Please," she said, "what do you call this valley?"

The old man looked surprised and amused. "I call it nothing. It is simply my valley. But I have heard others name it." He gave the companions an unreadable smile. "I have heard it called Shangri-la."

He turned and set off up the hills surrounding the valley, leaving Jack, Merle, and Loaf to recover from their astonishment and scramble hastily in his footsteps.

Tingkat gazed down into the valley with a grim smile of satisfaction.

It had taken her most of the day to find. *It was unlikely,* she thought, *that the inhabitants of this primitive world knew that such a place existed*. Even the sophisticated instruments on her stolen ship had scanned this region three times before she had spotted the subtle signs of its presence. Now she stood on a ledge several hundred feet above the valley and watched through the gathering dusk as the humans and their companions followed a slim, robed figure up from the valley.

Tingkat lowered her longsight viewer. This time, there would be no low-tech weapons to get in her way, no interfering bounty hunters, no inconvenient so-called gods. This time, she only had to overcome the guardians of The Server and a feeble old man. This time, she would not fail.

Her wrist communicator buzzed. She answered it, and a familiar harsh voice spoke. "Do you have The Server?"

"I shall," grated Tingkat. "Soon."

"No." The Tyrant's tone did not encourage argument. "I have another task for you."

"But The Server . . ."

"I have other plans for The Server. Return to your ship. Await further instructions. Acknowledge."

Tingkat gritted her teeth. "Very well."

She broke the connection. For a moment she stood, undecided. Then she took the communicator from her wrist and hurled it away from her. It fell for a long time, turning and glinting in the rays of the setting sun.

With catlike agility, the bounty hunter continued her descent into the hidden valley.

The last of the light was draining from the sky by the time the companions and their guide reached the small shrine that stood on bare rock at the head of the valley.

It was simply a standing stone, of about shoulder height, with a niche carved in it. Small offerings lay in the niche and on the rocks at its foot. A handful of grains, hair braided together to make a bracelet, polished stones. The old man indicated the offerings. "Men and women still come up here. Sometimes they leave food or pieces of cloth. They believe such gifts bring them good luck." He smiled enigmatically. "Perhaps they do." He said nothing more but indicated the shrine with a wave of his wrinkled hand and stepped back.

Jack nodded. He felt there was a lot to be learned from this apparently defenseless stranger who had managed to create a small paradise from a terrible wilderness. But they had things to do and no time to waste. He stepped forward and opened The Server. "Help."

Their guide showed no sign of surprise or emotion as the hologram materialized above The Server's keyboard. "Yeah?" growled Help with his customary lack of charm. But even the cranky hologram sounded less aggressive than usual. It was as if no quarrel could take hold in the world of the valley.

Wordlessly, Jack pointed at the shrine. Without comment, Help materialized his sunglasses and sent out a beam of ultrared that washed across the stone, revealing only one symbol: a pair of interlocking comma shapes, one white with a black dot and one black with a white dot, which between them formed a circle.

"Science and magic," said the old man. "Mystery and knowledge. Dark and light." Once again, he gave a faint, enigmatic smile. "Friend and FOE." The companions stared at him. How could this hermit possibly know of the struggle for control of the whole Galaxy that was being played out among the stars? But the man only concluded, "Yin and yang. A circle is only complete when you return to where you began."

Jack nodded and reached out to touch the glowing symbol.

"Move one more muscle and you are a dead being."

Tingkat stepped forward from the darkness. She held an energy pistol in one hand. The other was held out for The Server. "No more speeches," said the bounty hunter. "The game ends here. Give me The Server, or die."

As Jack hesitated, the moon rose.

It emerged from behind the mountains that ringed the valley, and a change came over their guide. The stooped old figure grew and filled out. Its robes fell away, to be replaced by a heavy pelt of snow-white hair. Its gnarled hands became powerful, taloned paws. Its eyes burned. It lifted its arms, threw back its great head, and roared.

Bitz stared at the newly revealed creature openmouthed. "What do you know! The old guy's a shape-shifter like us."

"Nice transformation," agreed Googie. "Maximum points for style, scariness, and technical merit."

Tingkat's mouth dropped open. Even in her adventurous existence, the bounty hunter had never witnessed such a metamorphosis. By the time she had recovered, it was already too late. The bearlike creature, now more than nine feet tall, moved with incredible speed to smash Tingkat's weapon. It roared again, a roar that echoed around the encircling mountains and was answered by the thunder of an unseen avalanche. Tingkat gave a strangled cry of fear, took to her heels, and ran, with the creature in pursuit.

Loaf's mouth looked like a door that someone had forgotten to close. "Did everyone see what I just saw?" The others nodded, speechless. "What *was* that thing?"

Jack said, "I saw a TV program once about mystery beasts — you know, the Loch Ness monster, Bigfoot, things like that. They mentioned a creature that lived in the Himalayas. It was called the abominable snowman. At least, that's what mountaineers called it. The local people called it the yeti."

Loaf's eyes boggled. "That was a yeti?"

Jack shrugged. "Whatever it was, it's given us the chance we need to get out of here." Without hesitation, he reached for the center of the yin-yang symbol and pushed.

Stonehenge, Salisbury Plain, England

The sun was once more sinking in the west when the companions found themselves standing inside a great circle of standing stones.

"Stonehenge," said Merle.

Jack nodded. "The old man said, 'A circle is only complete when you return to where you began.' There must be one more thing we have to do to complete the Chain."

"Indeed." A hooded figure stepped from behind one of the great stones. "Such a pity you will not have the chance to do it."

"Yo, dudes and dudettes!" A figure in flamboyant but tattered clothes stepped from the opposite side of the circle. "Long time, no see!"

"Zodiac Hobo!" snarled Bitz.

Googie yowled deep in her throat. "And Tracer!"

CHAPTER NINE

Merle gave Zodiac a killing look. "I thought you said you didn't work for the FOEs."

Zodiac spread his hands in a gesture of helplessness. "Hey, man, don't get heavy with me. I got to work for somebody."

Jack looked steadily at Tracer. "Why should we hand The Server over to you?" he demanded.

"Because of this." With one of his claws, Tracer pulled out an energy weapon that he had held concealed behind his back. "Of course," he continued in apologetic tones, "it's only a hand weapon — not very big or powerful. But it's more than you have."

"T-mail us out of here, Jack," hissed Merle.

"To where, exactly?" Tracer's ears twitched.

Merle realized that she had underestimated the sensitivity of the alien's hearing. "You've already visited all the ancient sites on Earth and activated their defenses — thereby, incidentally, ensuring that they will not receive any further incoming teleports. And you dare not teleport yourselves offworld." Tracer gave an unpleasant chuckle. "I believe you have been guilty of what your species figuratively calls getting stuck at a dead end. Or to put it more crudely, you're out of options." The weapon in Tracer's claw pointed unwaveringly at Merle. He held two more claws out toward Jack. "Give me The Server."

Bitz gave a yap of dismay. "Don't do it, Jack."

"Jack!" yelled Merle. "Don't worry about me!"

"No," said Loaf, eyeing Tracer's pistol nervously. "Worry about how he'll probably shoot me after he's shot her. That's what *I'm* worried about."

Merle waved frantically at Jack. "Get out of here! He thinks if he threatens me, you'll do what he wants."

Jack looked from Merle to Tracer and back again. "The trouble is," he said. He hesitated. "The trouble is," he began again, "he's right."

Googie hissed. "You humans are such sentimentalists!"

"Jack!" Merle was beside herself with rage. "If you even think about giving this creep The Server because of what he might do to me, I'll never speak to you again!"

Jack shrugged. "If I don't give him The Server, you won't be able to." He placed The Server on one of the fallen stones and stepped back.

Merle gave a hollow groan. "Jack, I'm not speaking to you — except for speaking to you now to tell you that I'm not speaking to you."

Tracer stepped forward. The energy pistol remained trained on Merle as he stooped and gathered The Server into his arms. "At last." He breathed. "So long in the planning — and now, the endgame begins." With two more of his claws, the elephant-eared being began to tap a complex series of instructions into the keyboard.

Bitz pawed at Jack's leg for attention. "Remember what Janus said? We can't let him try to teleport out of here. Whatever destination he selects, he's going to wind up t-mailing himself right into The Tyrant's rumpus room with The Server."

Jack nodded grimly. "I know. But there's nothing we can do."

Tracer's expression as he turned to Jack was a strange mixture of wry amusement and resignation, mingled with something else — it might almost have been anticipation, even triumph. But, Jack reminded himself, he really wasn't very good at reading alien expressions.

"Kind of you to be concerned," said Tracer softly, "but I am not altogether a fool. I know what I'm doing." He looked around at the silent companions: at Jack, who was watching him stony faced; at Bitz, whose muzzle was drawn back in a snarl; at Googie, whose cat face was inscrutable; at Loaf, slouching moodily; at Merle, who was regarding him with hatred, tears of frustration welling in her dark eyes. With a return to his old manner, Tracer winked at them. "It's been fun." He held up The Server and prepared to press the SEND key.

Just then, a shadow fell across the ancient stones. Startled, Tracer looked up.

Zodiac's ship had stolen upon them silently and was now hovering above Stonehenge, almost touching the tops of the mighty stones of the inner circle. As Tracer gaped, a hatch shot open in *Trigger*'s belly. A flexible cargo-handling arm shot out. The handlike mechanism at its tip swooped with the speed of a striking snake and pinned Tracer against one of the great standing stones.

Loaf let out a whoop of malicious delight. "How d'ya like them apples, Dumbo? Awesome! *Trigger* to the rescue!"

Tracer scrabbled furiously at the metallic claw with the three of his hands that were not otherwise occupied. "What is it doing? Has it gone mad? Hobo! Call your ship off!"

Zodiac looked as if he was trying hard not to grin. "Hey, man, sorry — like, I must have left it on automatic pilot." He raised his voice. "*Trigger!* C'mon, baby! Let the dude go, will ya?"

"No!" *Trigger*'s amplified electronic voice was uncompromising. "I don't like him. He's not a nice being."

Zodiac shrugged. "Y'know, I ain't crazy about the guy myself, but . . ."

"He said I was stupid!" snapped *Trigger*. "He called me an idiot machine. He said I was operationally challenged, and he was amazed I could fly. He made me fight that snake thing." *Trigger* shuddered. "And he made me go through that wormhole."

"Yeah, yeah." Zodiac waved his arms ineffectually. "But he owns you, see — I mean, like, I don't dig capitalism, but . . ."

"And he threatened the human, Merle," hissed *Trigger*. "She was kind to me. She treated me like a person. She gave me my name." *Trigger* squeezed the claw tighter. Tracer gave a squeak of dismay and wriggled furiously to get *his* claw on the SEND button. *Trigger* squeezed again. Tracer gasped and dropped his pistol — and The Server.

Merle stepped forward and picked up the gun. "Thank you, *Trigger*," she said in a voice that fought hard to stay calm. "You can let him go now."

"Awww!" The ship's voice was plaintive. "Can't I squeeze him some more?"

"No," said Merle firmly. "We'll deal with him now." Reluctantly, *Trigger* loosened its grip. The cargo arm snaked back into its bay,

and the hatch slid closed. But the ship remained at its post, humming faintly.

In its shadow, Jack stepped forward. Once
more he picked up The Server. He raised his
head and faced Tracer, who was rubbing his
bruised chest with all six claws (this was a
rather disturbing sight), still gasping for breath.

"There's been a change of plan." Jack
tapped slowly at The Server's keys. Tracer
eyed him with apprehension.

Merle said, "Do you want me to do that?"

Jack shook his head. "Keep him covered.
This is my responsibility. I won't ask anyone
else to do it." Tracer's apprehension was
clearly turning to alarm.

Jack finished inputting instructions. "The
Server is all set." He looked Tracer straight in
the visor. "Where would you like to go?"

Tracer's visor flashed erratically. "You're
letting me go?"

"Sure. I'm going to t-mail you out of here,
like you wanted. There's just one small adjust-
ment to your plan. You're not taking The
Server."

"No!" Tracer's voice was almost a shriek.
"You don't understand!"

"Arcadia?" asked Jack. "I hear it's very nice at this time of year. Of course, it doesn't really matter where you choose to go."

Tracer licked his dry lips. In a voice that was no more than a whisper, he said, "Listen to me. Please. You can't send me to The Tyrant without The Server."

"I daresay he'll be disappointed," admitted Jack. His voice was calm, but his expression was as hard as flint. He went on, "I'm only sending you back where you belong. The Tyrant should be pleased with you. You've tried to take The Server from us. You used the MindMelt on Loaf."

"Yeah!" said Loaf, rubbing his neck and giving Tracer a resentful look.

"You sent the Bug that took Janus into N-space and the one that turned Merle's dad into a zombie. You let the Collectors torture Tiresias. You threatened to shoot Merle." Jack gave Tracer an icy smile. "You can tell The Tyrant that you tried your best. I'm sure you'll be able to explain." His finger jabbed down on the SEND key.

Tracer's face was a picture of horror and dismay. Even as blue-white light surrounded him and the forces of the teleportation event disassembled his body molecule from molecule, his despairing cry echoed around the stones of the circle.

"You fool! What have you done?"

And then he was gone.

Jack's shoulders drooped. He sighed.

"Yeah! Great going, Jack! That got the creep off our backs. I hope The Tyrant tears him to pieces!" Loaf gave a jubilant cackle and thumped Jack on the arm.

"Shut up, Loaf," said Jack.

Loaf stared at him. "What'd I say?"

"Like I said," drawled Googie, "humans are sentimentalists. He's getting a guilt complex because he sent Tracer back to The Tyrant."

Loaf snorted. "Sap."

Merle gazed uneasily through a wide gap at the southwestern quadrant of the stone circle. "Guys, I think we'd better move fast."

The sky was nearly dark. The friends gazed around at bright specks of light converging quickly on the stone circle.

"Bounty hunters," snapped Bitz. "At least fifty of them. T-mailing Tracer out of here must have given them a fix on us. We have to find the last symbol and activate the Chain — fast, before they get here."

Jack nodded. "Help."

Help appeared. "Well, lookie here!" said the hologram snidely. "Guess where we are again. You primates can't hardly stay away from this place."

"Not now," said Jack. "We have one more symbol to find, and we don't have much time to scan the stones."

"We don't need to," said Help smugly. "I was paying attention when we were last here, even if you weren't. The last symbol is here." The now familiar purple-red light appeared as a tight beam that rested on a massive fallen stone. As the companions watched, a strange picture appeared — a glowing serpent, bent into the shape of an *O*, swallowing its own tail.

The whine of the bounty hunters' approaching craft was building to a scream.

Merle reached out and traced the outline of the snake. "'A circle is only complete when you return to where you began.'" She nodded, as if seeing the solution to a puzzle. "The ouroboros."

Loaf stuck a finger in his ear and wiggled it. "Say what?"

"Oo-rob-or-ross," said Merle slowly. She caught Loaf's confused stare and rolled her eyes. "Later." With her hand hovering over the symbol, Merle gave Jack an enquiring look. He nodded.

The bounty hunters closed in. Merle pressed the button.

There was a flare of blue-white light from every stone at once, brighter than ever before. The circle of light expanded, racing away to every horizon.

Every time it touched a bounty hunter's ship, the vessel was bathed in light and vanished as suddenly and completely as a soap bubble. Only *Trigger* — protected, Jack thought, by its position at the heart of the circle — remained.

Then there was silence. The hum of the stones dropped until it was barely audible. Nevertheless, there was a strange air of watchfulness in the ancient circle, as if, at any moment, the power of the stones could flare up again, to drive away any invader.

Loaf was still staring around in amazement. He turned to Jack and Merle.

"But —" He moistened his lips and began again. "All those bounty hunters. Where did they *go*?"

Unknown Planet

A bounty hunter stepped out of its crippled craft, energy weapon at the ready. It gazed apprehensively around at the strange and sinister jungle surrounding it. Horrible noises — shrieks, squawks, roars, and snarls — sounded from all sides. Bushes shook.

It spotted a fellow bounty hunter backing away from its own useless vessel. They moved cautiously through the undergrowth until they stood back-to-back.

"What is this planet?" whispered the first bounty hunter.

"Aaaaaargh!" replied the second bounty hunter.

The first bounty hunter felt an ice-cold chill run down its spine. "Do you mean the planet Aaaaaargh, with six *a*'s, home to the eyeball-popping razor-toothed ear-driller and the most horrifyingly dangerous place in the known Galaxy?"

There was no reply. The second bounty hunter fell to the damp earth with a thump.

The first bounty hunter gulped. "I'll take that as a yes, then."

Stonehenge, Salisbury Plain, England

"The ouroboros," said Merle as they stood and watched the symbol fade back into the ancient stone, "is old. Nobody knows quite how old. It occurs all over the world — Egypt, Greece, Iran, you name it. It's the symbol of eternal life — constant renewal. An endless cycle of existence."

Jack nodded. "Like the yin-yang."

"And like the *O* of Outernet," added Bitz.

"Like the ring of a doughnut," said Loaf. In the silence that followed this remark, the others stared at him. Loaf looked uncomfortable. "I'm taking kind of a lateral approach to this analogy."

"Well, the Outernet as we know it won't last forever," said Jack. "Not if The Tyrant gets his way. But I guess that's sort of out of our hands now. The Server should be safe here on Earth. By circling the globe and activating each site, we've put the Chain in place. Janus said nobody can break it."

An owl hooted. The air was getting colder. Merle shivered. "We didn't find The Weaver," she said. "But maybe we did enough. Don't you think so?"

Jack shrugged. "I don't know."

Merle moved closer to Jack. "Say, you know what you did back there? When you gave Tracer The Server so he wouldn't shoot me?"

Jack looked at his feet.

"That was" — Merle's voice was husky — "that was . . ."

Jack waited.

Merle swallowed hard. "That was . . . really stupid."

Jack gave a shout of laughter. Then he cupped his hands and called to the ship that was still hovering over the stone circle, "Hey, *Trigger*! Could you give us a lift?"

Zodiac looked alarmed. "Hey, sorry, dude. Like, I'll be in enough trouble with The Tyrant when Tracer tells him what happened here without giving you guys a ride. Company policy, man — no unauthorized passengers."

"Shut up!" *Trigger's* voice snapped, silencing Zodiac. "Of course. I'll be happy to give you a ride," *Trigger* went on in gentler tones. "I'll enjoy having some polite, civilized company aboard for once. It will be my pleasure."

"Oh, man," groaned Zodiac. "Even my ship gives me a hard time."

Jack turned to the others and said quietly, "Let's go home."

CHAPTER TEN

Little Slaughter,
near Cambridge, England

"Well, dudes and dudette," drawled Zodiac, "it looks like it's the end of the road. Me and *Trigger* are gonna hightail it off this planet once and for all and head for the stars. Like they say: To infinity!"

"And beyond?" suggested Loaf.

Zodiac looked puzzled. "Heck, no. What sort of crazy idea is that? There's nothing beyond infinity!"

The journey from Stonehenge had taken just a few minutes. *Trigger* had crept in under the air base radar and landed just outside the village of Little Slaughter in order to avoid prying eyes and further missile greetings from the United States Air Force.

The friends stood at the bottom of the

ship's landing ramp. Zodiac was at the top, his body outlined by the cabin lights.

"Good-bye, Merle," sniffed *Trigger*. "Thank you again for my name. I'll miss you."

Merle gave a nod. "Same here," she said awkwardly.

The ship burst into electronic sobs. Merle shuffled her feet in embarrassment. Having only suggested the name *Trigger* as a joke, she couldn't help feeling that she didn't really deserve the ship's high regard.

Zodiac gave his battered vessel a pained look. "Oh, man, that's all I need, an emotional wreck of a ship!" He jabbed at a button. "Come on, *Trigger*, pull yourself together." The landing ramp retracted into the ship.

Jack gave Zodiac a final wave. "Thank you for everything you've done."

"In spite of trying not to," muttered Loaf under his breath.

"No problemo, amigos. It's been a blast." Zodiac thought for a second. "Mostly." He thought again. "Well, it's been weird." He gave a theatrical salute. "Plant you now, dig you later."

Loaf frowned. "Say what?"

"I think he's saying good-bye," explained Googie.

"Right on, wild child." The door closed with a quiet *shoosh*.

Trigger's engines coughed to life, and within seconds the ship lifted into a night sky that glistened and shimmered with the light of a million stars.

Trigger gave a farewell barrel roll and shot upward. The companions watched in silence as the ship grew smaller and smaller before disappearing into the vastness of space.

"Do you think we'll ever see them again?" Merle wondered out loud.

"If we're particularly unlucky," said Googie.

Jack shrugged. "Who knows?"

"And who cares?" said Loaf.

"You don't mean that!" Merle scolded.

"Why not?" replied Loaf. "I'm getting tired of all this saving the Galaxy stuff. It's about time we started showing some concern for *us*. And I'm starting with getting some good food inside my belly. I haven't eaten for hours."

Merle flicked open her cell phone. "I'll call my dad and see if we can get a ride."

Jack put his hand over the phone mouthpiece. "Merle, if your dad gets hold of me, he'll lock The Server up in the most bombproof vault he can find and hang on to me for questioning for who knows how long. Listen. I'll come to the base and talk to your dad tomorrow. I promise. But right now, I just want to go home and see *my* mum and dad. You lost me somewhere on the trail. You don't know where I am. Okay?"

Bitz gave a nod. "Me, too. I'm not going back to that pound! There's a Doberman I do not want to see again."

Googie arched her back against Merle's legs. "I'd better lie low as well. Now that your father knows I can talk, I don't think he'll be quite as relaxed as he used to be about finding me asleep on his confidential files."

Merle nodded. "Okay. See you soon." She turned to Loaf. "I suppose you want a ride?" she said without enthusiasm.

Loaf gave her a hard stare. "Don't knock yourself out."

As Jack, Bitz, and Googie walked off, fading into the darkness, Merle dialed and held the phone to her ear. "Kirk to *Enterprise*, two to beam up. Oh, sorry, Dad, just fooling around. Where am I? I'm back. Listen, I know it's pretty late, but could you do me a really *big* favor?"

U.S. Air Force Base, Little Slaughter, near Cambridge, England

Merle and Loaf sat at the breakfast table in Colonel Stone's kitchen. Major Jackson leaned against the refrigerator. Merle's father paced up and down the vinyl floor, his forehead creased in thought.

On their arrival at the base, Merle and her father had done a lot of hugging, and Loaf's father had done a lot of shouting before turning Loaf over to Colonel Stone for a debrief. "Give him the third degree," the master sergeant had growled. "Be my guest." But Loaf had refused to say anything until he'd had at least two double cheeseburgers with fries. These had been ordered from the nearest snack bar. Loaf was currently polishing off burger number two. Merle was picking at a pasta salad and relating, between mouthfuls, the events of the past hours.

As she reached the end of the story, Colonel Stone shook his head. "Incredible." He turned to Major Jackson. "We keep this to ourselves — for tonight." He gave Merle and Loaf a stern look. "But tomorrow, the formalities start. You say you don't know where your friend Jack is right now?"

"Haven't a clue," said Merle truthfully. After all, he could be anywhere in Little Slaughter at this *exact* moment.

"We'll need to talk to him — and those two aliens. Especially the one that keeps sharpening her claws on my desk. You're going to have to tell the whole thing again, and not to me and the major here. There are some people from the Pentagon and a special agency jetting across the Atlantic to talk to all of you."

"Will they be wearing black suits and cool sunglasses?" asked Loaf hopefully.

Colonel Stone raised an eyebrow. "I think that dress code is purely for the movies and television."

Loaf seemed disappointed. "Too bad."

Merle's father sighed. "You should have tried to detain this Zobo character for questioning. He could have been real useful in determining threat estimates from Alien Life-Forms."

"But, Dad," objected Merle with wide-eyed innocence, "he's a space desperado, a real dangerous character. You wouldn't have wanted us to put ourselves in more danger, would you?"

"I guess not." Colonel Stone frowned. "And no talking to the press. There's been a lot of interest in the past couple days' events."

"Has it made TV? Are we celebrities?" asked Loaf hopefully.

Major Jackson shook his head. "There's been a press blackout. All the activity with the hunters was called an important military exercise. National security has been cited. The fuss will die down."

"But what about all the people who saw the Sphinx and the flying snake?" said Loaf. "What are they saying?"

"Apparently the special agency I mentioned has sent agents to track down and talk to the people," continued Major Jackson.

"Are they all having their memories erased with flashy things?" asked Loaf.

"You *do* watch too many movies," replied the colonel. "I'm not aware that we have that technology. It's more a case of confiscating photos and videos."

"You mean," said Merle incredulously, "the government is trying to explain away something that was seen by thousands of people?"

"It wouldn't be the first time," replied Stone acidly. "It's been spread around that there is something funky going on with the Cairo water supply. The authorities in Mexico are putting out some story about a couple of experimental airplanes involved in the capture of a runaway weather balloon."

"Weather balloon?" Merle asked mockingly. "They'll never believe that!"

"They always have before. Heck, if we can get away with Roswell, we can get away with anything."

Loaf moaned. "So no one is going to know how we saved the Galaxy?"

"We haven't yet," said Merle. "The Weaver still doesn't have The Server."

"That isn't your responsibility anymore," said Colonel Stone. "It's up to the U.S. government to decide how we should take up the fight with this Tyrant." He rubbed his eyes. "Okay. We've all been keeping late hours recently. I guess anything else can wait until tomorrow. The boys from across the pond won't be here until then." He pointed at Merle. "You, get to bed." He pointed at Loaf. "You — just get."

3 The Almshouses, Little Slaughter, near Cambridge, England

"Mum! Dad!" Jack called out. "I'm home!" He pushed through the front door to his house and walked into the lounge. "Mum! Dad!"

There was no reply. Puzzled, Jack wandered into the kitchen. Bitz trotted behind. Googie had decided to prowl around the garden, looking for small furry things to chase. Jack had complained that this was cruel. Googie had said she was tired of being hunted. She thought she owed herself a change of role. Jack was too tired to argue.

He flung open the door to the living room. "Hi! It's me!" Still nothing. Strange. Maybe they were in bed — after all, it was late. He ran upstairs and knocked on his parents' bedroom door. Silence. Hardly daring to breathe, Jack pushed the door open. The room was empty.

Panic flooded through his body. He ran from room to room. No lights, no sound — nothing.

"Where are they?" Jack's voice cracked.

"Stay calm!" Bitz gave Jack a worried look. "Maybe they went to a restaurant or a movie."

"They don't do that!" snapped Jack. "Mum! Dad!"

"Shhh!" growled Bitz. "You want to wake the whole neighborhood?"

Fighting down his terror, Jack put The Server on the kitchen table. As he did so, his attention was drawn to what appeared to be a piece of grass lying on the polished wood. Jack wondered how it had gotten there. He picked it up. His legs turned to rubber and his heart missed a beat. It wasn't grass. It was a strand of hair. Spiky green hair.

Bitz whined. "I hope that isn't what I think it is."

Ching!

Help materialized from The Server. Its usual jaunty manner was gone. "Don't shoot me — I'm just the messenger." Jack stared at the hologram with dread. "You've got mail, and you ain't gonna like it." Help disappeared back into The Server.

Jack took a deep breath and clicked on the o-mail icon.

From: *The Tyrant*
Subject: *Bait*

Human:
I am tired of playing games.
You have something that I want very badly.
I have something you want — your parents.
You will use t-mail, and I will divert you to my headquarters.
You will bring The Server with you.
If you do not, then your parents will suffer.
Do this immediately.
The Tyrant

Jack sat down on a kitchen chair. In his mind's eye, he could see what had happened — Tingkat arriving at the house, kidnapping his parents, and then teleporting to The Tyrant's lair.

Bitz put a comforting paw on his knee. "Gee, Jack, I'm sorry."

Jack ruffled the dog's ears absentmindedly. "That settles it," he said. "I didn't know where to go next. Now I do." He ran his fingers over the scuffed case of The Server. "I'm going to get my mum and dad back. I'm going to The Tyrant."

There's something out there . . .
And it's the next

#6 weaver

"To get to the Bugs," said Help, "we may have to face the most terrible creature in the known Galaxy. The legendary space-dwelling monster, Wiggly Woo."

Loaf stared wide-eyed at Help. "Wiggly Woo?"

Help nodded. "The Cosmic leviathan. The Great White Worm."

"Aaarrrccchh," said Zodiac, gasping like a fish out of water.

"Wiggly Woo?"

"The beast that cannot be chained. Terror of the spaceways. Swallower of fleets."

"*Wiggly Woo?*" Loaf wiped a trembling hand across his eyes. "Let me get this straight. You had to think of a name for the hugest and most terrifying creature in the entire Galaxy. You had billions of names, in billions of languages to choose from. And the name you came up with was WIGGLY WOO?"

"A name to strike dread into the strongest heart or other circulatory organ," agreed Help in hushed tones. "In the language of Auriga III it means, 'The Mighty Destroyer, Ship Crusher, Star Shaker, Deep-Dwelling Scourge of the Cosmos, Maker Of Widows (Or Widowers, Obviously) And Orphans.'"

"That's an awful lot for Wiggly Woo to mean," drawled Googie.

"Aurigan is a very compact language." Help gave her a patronizing smile.

"But it's a joke name," Loaf was still protesting, "out of a stupid kids' rhyme!"

"You see?" demanded Help triumphantly. "Even on Earth, which has no contact with the rest of the Galaxy, trembling mothers sing to their children, warning them of the danger of the Enormous Squirmy One." Help began to sing in an off-key, creaky voice. *"There's a worm at the bottom of the wormhole, and his name is Wiggly Woo."*

"It's 'There's a worm at the bottom of my garden,'" began Merle, "and I'm sure they're not talking about the same —"

Zodiac, finally finding his voice, interrupted her. "Hoooold on there, dude! Are you crazy?" The space hippie pointed a grubby finger at Help. "Are you out of your cybernetic mind? There's no way this cat is going back through no wormhole, you dig? Like, forget it, man! Nix, nerts, *n-o* spells no!"

"I won't do it!" *Trigger*'s artificial voice cracked with hysteria. "You can't make me face the worms again! The wriggliness. The slime. The teeth! Oooooh!" The ship's voice rose to an electronic scream.

"*Trigger*!" Merle's sharp voice cut through the ship's wail. *Trigger* quieted, still sniffling. Merle turned to Help. "Is there any way we could get to the Bugs in time to save Jack's mom and dad, without going through the wormhole?"

Help shook his head. "I'm afraid not. I'm frightfully sorry."

"Okay," said Merle. Her voice dropped, sounding like the kind of coo a turtle dove might use on its mate if it had forgotten their anniversary. "*Trigger.*"

"Merle, please," *Trigger* said tearfully, "don't make me do it. You know I'll do it for you, so don't ask, please, because it's really not a good idea and I'm so scared."

Merle stroked the instrument panel that housed *Trigger*'s electronic brain. "We're all scared, honey," she murmured. "I hate to ask, but you heard Help. There just isn't any other way."

"Oh, all right!" snapped *Trigger*, firing up its main engines with an unnecessary burst of revs. "But when you're swallowed by a mouth the size of a planet, and chewed to a paste by teeth bigger than mountains, and dissolved into chemical soup by a cloud of seething energized gasses millions of miles across in a stomach that could swallow a star — don't come crying to me!"

Trigger shot away from the station into deep space, searching for the swirling pattern of cosmic radiation that would mark the entrance to a wormhole.

"You never know," said Zodiac nervously. "We could get lucky." He stared out at the spiraling whirlpool of energy and sparkling matter that marked the mouth of the wormhole into which

Trigger was speeding at whoosh factor six. "Some wormholes are just a straight here-to-there deal, y'know? The worst we're likely to see in them would be itty-bitty worms only a couple hundred miles long." The space desperado used a grease-stained bandanna to wipe sweat from his forehead.

"Is this that kind of wormhole?" asked Loaf, peering anxiously through the window on the opposite side of *Trigger*'s cramped flight deck.

"Nope," said Bitz regretfully, punching controls with his paws. "Scans indicate that this is one of the other kind."

"And what happens in the other kind?" asked Merle in an I-don't-think-I'm-going-to-like-the-answer-to-this voice.

"Well," squeaked Zodiac, "in the other kind, you come to some type of a, like, central hub where there are lots of other wormholes, and you have to cross the hub and go through another wormhole to get to the end."

"And that is bad," prompted Merle, "because . . . ?"

"Because the area in the middle of the wormholes is where Wiggly Woo lives."

The spinning jaws of the wormhole rushed to meet them.

Zodiac hid his head in his hands. "Oh maaaaaaaaan!"

About the Authors

Steve Barlow and Steve Skidmore

Steve and Steve are both humans of an indeterminate age who have been writing books for young life-forms for more than thirteen Earth years. They live in England with their pets, families, and other aliens. They are presently working on the Zargian version of Outernet but are finding the spelling very difficult.

About the Website

About You and the Outernet

Once you've logged on to the Outernet, use this space to record your identification.

AGENT ID   _____

PASSWORDS _____

_____

_____

OUTERNET

FROM: The Weaver (address unknown)
TO: New Outernet User

RE: Security Breach

Greetings, unidentified life-form. Mel, a DRAMA official,
has discovered your download and has tracked it to this location.
He has already told a huge FIB agent that you – and possibly
your friends – now know of the existence of the Outernet.
Because the Forces of Evil also may have located
you – we see no alternative but to recruit you.

Proceed directly to the link below to:

• Report to FIB and become a Friends Agent with your own secret identity
• Take part in top secret missions to defeat the Forces of Evil (FOEs)
• Send and receive Outernet mail with other Friends on the Outernet
• Explore alien sites and gather more information on individuals
and their worlds

Good luck, Friend, and remember…Preserve your Link…Maintain the Chain.

www.go2outer.net